## Holy. Hell.

Damon stopped on the stone driveway leading down to the wrought iron gate.

A woman stood outside the heavy bars, her fingers clutching the filigree that surrounded the house number in the center of the entrance. She was the right height. Even from this distance, he could recognize those dark brown eyes. The delectably full lips. The hair that had once been sun-streaked blond was now a shade of honey-gold pinned back in a way that showed hollows under cheeks formerly rounded with good health. Her frame was thinner. Her skin paler. And her expression was wary, lacking the vibrant self-confidence of the capable businesswoman he remembered.

Yet there wasn't a single doubt in his mind.

"Caroline."

He forced himself into motion again, even though he had no idea what he would say to his long-lost wife.

\* \* \*

*Claiming His Secret Heir* is part of the McNeill Magnates trilogy: Those McNeill men just have a way with women.

Dear Reader,

Fasten your seat belts... I've got a roller-coaster ride for you this month! *Claiming His Secret Heir* is full of twists and surprises along with a heartfelt romance. This story gripped me from the moment I penned the heroine standing outside the gates of what should have been her home. I couldn't write the book fast enough because each day, I couldn't wait to see what happened next.

Truly, Damon and Caroline had their own stories to tell! I felt like I was just there to write down what happened. That's a rare and fun occurrence for an author, and has only happened to me a handful of times over the course of my career. Now I only hope I did a good enough job that you feel the same way I did—that you are turning pages to see what happens next!

Come, fall in love again...and enjoy the ride.

Happy reading,

*Joanne Rock*

# JOANNE ROCK

———

# CLAIMING HIS SECRET HEIR

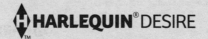

Recycling programs
for this product may
not exist in your area.

ISBN-13: 978-1-335-97126-5

Claiming His Secret Heir

Copyright © 2018 by Joanne Rock

**HARLEQUIN®**
™ www.Harlequin.com

**Printed in U.S.A.**

Four-time RITA® Award nominee **Joanne Rock** has penned over seventy stories for Harlequin. An optimist by nature and a perpetual seeker of silver linings, Joanne finds romance fits her life outlook perfectly— love is worth fighting for. A former Golden Heart® Award recipient, she has won numerous awards for her stories. Learn more about Joanne's imaginative Muse by visiting her website, joannerock.com, or following @joannerock6 on Twitter.

### Books by Joanne Rock

#### Harlequin Desire

##### *Bayou Billionaires*

*His Secretary's Surprise Fiancé*
*Secret Baby Scandal*

##### *The McNeill Magnates*

*The Magnate's Mail-Order Bride*
*The Magnate's Marriage Merger*
*His Accidental Heir*
*Little Secrets: His Pregnant Secretary*
*Claiming His Secret Heir*

Visit her Author Profile page at Harlequin.com, or joannerock.com, for more titles.

To you. Yes, you, my reader.
Thank you for choosing this book to read,
and for spending some of your valuable time
with me. Whether you're reading one of
my stories for the first time, or you've read
many of my books over the years,
I appreciate you more than I can say.
I hope our shared love of romance brings
us together again down the road.

# One

Steeling herself against the January chill, Caroline Degraff stood outside the gates of the Los Altos Hills mansion that would have been hers and wondered how to get in.

Her grip tightened on the wrought iron fence separating her from the French château-style home she'd helped to design but never lived in. Caroline guessed that she would already be visible on the property's security footage. Too late to turn back now from this crazy idea to show up unannounced.

Prepared to deceive the husband she'd once loved.

But she had to know the truth about the powerful man on the other side of this imposing enclosure dotted with motion-detecting cameras. The man she'd married eleven months ago but hadn't seen since their honeymoon, tech company mogul Damon McNeill. Her father, a well-known investor in Silicon Valley projects, had hated Damon even before the marriage. He'd sent Caroline into Damon's California-based social media software business, Transparent, as an entrepreneur in residence—a common practice in tech start-ups that could benefit from an outside business perspective—in the hope she'd find weaknesses Damon's investors could use to oust him from the CEO position. Except Caroline had fallen in love with Damon rather than give her father the scathing scouting report he'd craved.

She hadn't known until that time in her life how cold and manipulative her father could be. He'd called Caroline a traitor and refused to attend the wedding, preventing anyone else in her family from doing so, as well. That had hurt her deeply, but she'd been so in love with Damon, it hadn't mattered. The weeks they'd spent together in Italy for their honeymoon had been the happiest days of her life.

Then she'd travelled briefly to London on her own after the honeymoon. From there things got fuzzy in her mind. She remembered she'd argued with Damon on the phone because she'd seen her father while she was in London. But she also remembered returning to this very house overlooking San Francisco Bay. She'd never even seen Damon that day, and she'd been trying not to notice too many details of their new, custom-built home so they could enjoy it together when he got home from work. Then, while she'd been staring out over the Bay, she'd heard him enter the house.

Only it hadn't been him. After that, her memories of the ordeal were totally blurry. But she knew that day had been the beginning of a months-long nightmare. She'd been kidnapped and held for a ransom Damon never paid. He'd never informed her father at all. He hadn't even reported her as missing; the story was absent from all the news sites she'd scoured online.

Grinding her teeth together, she felt the old signs of fear and claustrophobia, the racing heart and cold sweats. These were the physical symptoms of panic attacks she'd been working for weeks to overcome with the help of a good therapist. She still wasn't able to shake the effect of weeks spent scared and alone, captive in a remote village somewhere on the Baja Peninsula, with guards who treated her humanely enough, but never let her forget that they would kidnap one of her younger siblings, too, if she didn't do as she was told.

Thoughts of Damon rescuing her had gotten her through the nights. Along with the comforting knowledge of their child growing inside her. A child she hadn't even been able to tell him about before the abduction.

"Ma'am?" A young man called to her through the wrought iron fence, making Caroline jump back from the scrolled gate. "Can I help you? Is the call button acting up out there or is the main house not answering?"

Her heart thumped so fast and so hard she couldn't

speak for a moment. Everything felt frozen while her pulse rate skyrocketed and the guy with a man-bun, and carrying a pair of gardening clippers, came closer.

Who would ever believe she had graduated with honors from a prestigious East Coast business program when she couldn't even find her tongue to answer a simple question? Who would guess she'd helped her investor father to make millions on the two other tech start-ups she'd recommended he buy, back before her life fell apart?

These days, Caroline didn't even trust her memory of what happened yesterday, let alone last year. She'd been drugged a few times during her captivity with roofie-style pills that made past events fuzzy. Between that and vicious bouts of morning sickness, her health had been in serious decline by the time her captors rowed her out to a remote island and left her stocked with enough food for a month, unguarded and alone. Thankfully, the drugs hadn't harmed her baby, but she'd been too ill to try looking for help. When she'd regained enough strength to do so, just two months before her due date, a fisherman had found her and contacted her father.

"Ma'am?" The gardener tossed aside a handful of dead roses and set down his heavy trimmer. With just a tee on, he seemed oblivious to the chill in the air. "If you go around to the back entrance, I can let you in the service gate."

Caroline swallowed down the panic as she remembered her therapist's affirming words. *You are strong and capable. Trust your instincts.*

"Is Mr. McNeill home?" She had to see Damon. To learn for herself if he'd only married her to win a favorable review of his company for the sake of the investors. Was it just to cling to his CEO position for another year and keep control of Transparent?

Had her charismatic husband duped her completely, even going so far as to marry her for profit?

Or had her father been feeding her lies from the day he'd quietly brought her back to one of the family homes in Vancouver to deliver her baby? Damon had made it impossible for her to contact him directly—his cell phone was disconnected and he wasn't responding to emails. Calls to his office weren't returned, although she had been too afraid to leave her real name, worried her father would find out she'd gone behind his back and contacted her husband. All along, her father had insisted Damon wanted nothing to do with her, and her internet searches seemed to support that. Her father had shown her a tabloid article that speculated about how Damon's grandfather had recently required his heirs be married for one year to inherit a portion of the McNeill legacy. Caroline hadn't even known Damon was related to those McNeills, one of the richest families in New York, but now she wondered if their marriage had been purely for business reasons.

But she'd certainly discovered a few disconcerting clues in the last two weeks that made her think her father could be manipulating her. Transparent had a board meeting one week from now, and she wanted to learn the truth before her father maneuvered Damon out of his CEO position.

"I think Mr. McNeill is here today, but you need an appointment to see him." The gardener peered at her curiously, perhaps wondering why any guest of a multimillionaire tech genius would show up at the gate with no vehicle and dressed more like domestic help.

She'd debated her strategy until she felt ill about it. But there was no other way. Damon had abandoned the cell number she had for him and wasn't responding to her other attempts to contact him. He hadn't launched a public search for her or filed a missing person report. If it was just about her and their marriage—maybe Caroline would simply walk away and start over.

But she had their six-week-old son to think about. And if there was any chance that what she and Damon had shared was real, she needed to understand what happened. Why he was carrying on his life as if she'd never existed.

"He'll want to see me." She hoped. She didn't have to fake the nervous tremble of her fingers as she fumbled in the back pocket of faded jeans and removed the tattered piece of paper her sister had found hidden in their father's den. "I want to ask him about this."

The document looked like it had gone through the washer and dryer a few times. Or maybe it had fallen into the Pacific with her once, when she'd tried to escape her captors. Caroline genuinely didn't remember. She'd suffered amnesia during the ordeal, but her memories were coming back.

Not that Damon McNeill needed to know.

"A marriage certificate?" Squinting at the washed-out ink, the gardener scratched the spot under the man-bun, shifting the dark hair side-to-side. "For Mr. McNeill?"

"I'm Caroline Degraff." She pointed to the name on the second line, trying to recapture the sense of shock she'd felt when her sister first showed her the paper.

She hadn't recalled the marriage for weeks after her father rescued her, yet he'd never mentioned it until she confronted him. He'd tried to keep her isolated from her family so she wouldn't learn the truth. Her mother was dead, her younger brothers at boarding school and her sister had been at university in the States. What else had he kept from her about her marriage? About Damon? Her therapist had gently suggested that Caroline had been subjected to gaslighting.

The gardener's gaze flicked up from the paper. "You're Mr. McNeill's wife?"

Her throat went dry. She remembered enough about Damon to know he might never forgive her for this deception she had planned. But if he'd been the one tricking her into romance in the first place, what would it matter?

She was going to fake amnesia to find out what he had to say about her disappearance. She had to know for sure if her father had been lying to her about her husband.

"I'm honestly not sure." She allowed all the doubts and fears of the last months to come through in her voice. That much was not an act. "We'll have to ask him because…" She bit her lip and blinked back the swell of emotion before she spilled out a lie that was crucial to getting the answers she needed for her child. "I don't remember."

"What did you just say?" Damon McNeill pressed the pause button on the video he'd been watching on the big screen in the downstairs media room.

He'd asked not to be disturbed while he watched a hacker's demonstration of how to unlock the security on the software Damon's company was bringing to market in the spring. The hacker had found legitimate issues Damon's technical team would need to patch. If he asked his own staff to troubleshoot, he would have gotten thirty-page reports that gave him the all-clear to go into production. Ask a twenty-two-year-old who busted complex digital coding for the thrills and the cash? He got results in forty-eight hours.

Except he'd have to rewind the video to the start now, because he couldn't keep his focus on the demonstration when he was getting calls from the housekeeping service. Damn it. He'd only hired outside help to get the house ready to put on the market since he didn't want to keep the place he'd barely set foot in since construction had finished a year ago.

Caroline had loved their Los Altos Hills home, spending weeks with the architect to get the design just right. And yet she'd disappeared from the property mere hours after setting foot in it for the first time after it was completed. That was more than enough reason for him to want the house gone from his life forever.

"Mr. McNeill, there's a woman at the gate." The head of the maid service had arrived this morning to personally oversee the housecleaning and stage photos for the Realtor. "She says she's your wife."

The phone slid from his hand, dropping halfway down to the chair before Damon slapped at it, stopping the descent by pinning the cell to his chest.

He went motionless, holding the device in place while keeping his heart in his rib cage at the same time.

*What. The. Hell.*

"What kind of joke is this?" He knew Caroline couldn't be out there. He'd hired private investigators to find her. He'd paid a ransom to someone claiming to have kidnapped her. He'd searched half the world for her himself, convinced something had happened to her even though her wealthy and powerful father insisted Caroline had simply found Damon unsuitable and no longer wished to be married.

Stephan Degraff had said Caroline wished to travel and was entitled to her privacy, a story that was upheld by the occasional hits on her credit card. An apartment rented briefly in Prague. A used car purchased in Kiev.

Damon had never bought it.

He shot to his feet.

"No joke, sir." The housekeeper's voice was cool and modulated, as if she'd grown accustomed to disagreeable clients long ago. "She has a marriage certificate with your name on it and she looks like the photograph I'm staring at over the mantel. Shall we open the gate?"

Caroline on his doorstep after her father insisted she'd seen the error of her ways in marrying Damon and had walked out on him for good? Not damn well likely.

"I'll be right there." Damon was already charging toward the door. He shoved his way through with one shoulder. "Find the number for the local police, in case we need to send this crackpot a message about what happens to people who play pranks like impersonating my wife."

Cold fury roared through him. Caroline had been gone for ten and a half months. He'd chased false leads all over Europe, tracking withdrawals from her bank account and use of her credit card, trying to find her. All the while her father insisted she'd left her marriage and wished to be left alone. But then a ransom note had shown up weeks later, which he saw as proof she'd been kidnapped. But the police had never believed the kidnapping theory, insistent the ransom note was sent by someone who took advantage of her disappearance by demanding cash for her safe return.

Damon had gladly paid, transferring money to an offshore account on the appointed day. He'd never heard from the so-called kidnappers again.

Pounding his way up the stairs to the main floor, he couldn't wait to see who would have the nerve to pull a prank like this. He barreled through the handcrafted double doors that had delayed their move-in date by two weeks and stalked down the stone walkway covered in dried leaves that led to a fountain imported from India.

He hated all of it. And he rarely had an outlet for any of the fury that had seethed in him for weeks—fury that was a welcome change from the old fears for Caroline, the guilt that he hadn't done more to find her and the stark sense of loss...

*Holy. Hell.*

He stopped on the stone driveway leading down to the wrought iron gate.

A woman stood outside the heavy bars, her fingers clutching the filigree that surrounded the house number in the center of the entrance. She was the right height. Even from this distance, he could recognize those dark brown eyes. The delectably full lips. The hair that had once been sun-streaked blond was now a shade of honey gold and pinned back in a way that showed hollows under cheeks formerly rounded with good health. Her frame was thinner. Her skin paler. And her expression was wary, lacking the vibrant self-confidence of the capable businesswoman he remembered.

Yet there wasn't a single doubt in his mind.

Caroline Degraff had blindsided him the first time they met, igniting an incendiary passion that made him overlook every need for caution. Her father coveted Damon's company, but it didn't matter. Stephan Degraff had sent his smart, exquisite daughter to spy on Damon's operation, possibly to undermine him and oust him from his own company. But who cared? Damon would have given up everything—*everything*—to have Caroline.

Just when he'd thought he'd won her forever, after a honeymoon so beautiful that it hurt to recall, Caroline had vanished. She took her wallet and her car, a bag of clothes and a few prescription pills, all signs that, according to the cops, meant she left of her own volition. Her powerful father had convinced the police his daughter was entitled to her privacy and that she would file for divorce in her own time. The fact that Caroline left behind her wedding ring seemed to support the theory. Local law enforcement refused to file a missing person report, leaving Damon on his own to locate her. He'd been advised by multiple private investigators and the police not to talk to the media, so he hadn't. A story had been leaked to the press at one point, but her father had forced the news outlet to print a retraction. His lone effort to reach out to the public—discreetly asking for any information about her from the employees who had worked with them both at Transparent—had resulted in that ransom note.

Yet he never saw Caroline again.

Until now.

It occurred to him he'd stopped moving toward her. That he'd been staring at her like he'd seen a ghost for long, drawn-out moments, his head flooding with memories while his fingers ached with the need to touch her and see if she was real.

"Caroline." He forced himself into motion again, even though he had no idea what to say. Had she left him? Was she here for that divorce her father promised she would one day demand?

She backed up a step from the gate as he neared. She wore jeans with threadbare knees and faded thighs that hugged her subtle curves. A gray wool sweater with fat toggle buttons kept the chill out; the temperature was in the midfifties, with a cold breeze blowing off the bay. She wore no makeup, her face looking younger even as the expression in her eyes seemed far older than he remembered. She looked wary. Cautious.

And, if he read her expression correctly...confused. She appeared bewildered by his appearance even though *she* was the one who had shown up on *his* doorstep.

"Damon McNeill?" she asked, her arched eyebrows knitting together as she pursed her lips.

Just what the hell was she asking him? He noticed that one of the guys on the landscaping crew was hovering nearby, a crinkled piece of paper in his hand.

Damon pressed a button on his phone to open the electric gate and stared down the gardener while the bars slid silently to one side. "You can leave now. Water the roses or whatever."

"Sure thing." The guy nodded fast and seemed grateful for an excuse to leave, but first he ambled closer and handed Damon the faded, worn paper. "She said she found this."

Damon would have stuffed it in a back pocket to focus on Caroline, but the gold seal in one corner caught his eye.

Their marriage certificate.

"I don't understand." He moved closer to the wife who had once held his heart. The woman who now stared at him like a stranger. "Why did you bring this?"

His pulse pounded hard. He braced himself to hear the words he dreaded. The news that she wanted to end their marriage legally. Forever.

Alone on the private road that led to the mansion, she stuffed her hands in the pockets of the oversized sweater she wore, the fabric hugging her body tighter at the movement.

There'd been a time when he would have picked her up off her feet and wrapped her in both arms. Even not knowing where she'd been, what had happened or why she'd come back now, Damon still wanted to kiss her more than he wanted explanations. Something about her body language, so hesitant, restrained him.

"You're Damon." She seemed to seek confirmation, her brown eyes flecked with gold scanning his face, as if calculating the sum of his features. "I saw your photo online, but you look so much like your brother. Cameron."

*Half brother*, he silently corrected her while his brain tried to make meaning out of the nonsensical words.

"It's been less than a year since you saw me last. Do I look so different now?" He'd kissed her for long minutes in the airport in Florence, hating to part from her after the honeymoon. Their home in Los Altos Hills— this house—hadn't been completed yet. So she'd gone to see a friend in London while he flew back to the States for business that couldn't wait. Business he'd come to regret sorely in the last ten months, especially since they'd argued during the time they'd been apart and he'd always wondered if that had been the reason she left.

As it turned out, she hadn't just been seeing her friend, after all. She'd gone to the UK to make amends with her father, who would give anything to take control of Transparent. Stephan Degraff's plans to oust Damon were about to come to a head one week from now at the final board meeting before the product launched.

Had Caroline been helping her father take over Damon's company from the start?

"I don't remember." Her eyes were haunted. Scared. Unsure. "I've been in Mexico. With amnesia. I remembered my name two months ago, but it's taken time to recall more than that." She glanced up and away from him. Shut her eyes for a long moment before she began again. "I've had this paper ever since I woke up in a fishing village on the Baja Peninsula. But at the time, I didn't even know that name was mine."

Damon could not have been more stunned if she'd been the ghost he'd first imagined. Amnesia? A bracing gust of wind sucked the breath right out of him.

"You don't remember me? Us?" He tried to envision what this meant for them. Behind him, he heard the sprinkler system switch on.

"Nothing." She shook her head slowly, a wave of her honey-gold hair bumping her cheek. "I looked you up online weeks ago, but I've been scared to come because there was…no mention of me being missing. No photos of us together." She lifted her shoulders in an awkward shrug. "I thought maybe the marriage certificate was fake. Or that we divorced and you'd moved on—"

"No." He'd been living in a state of suspended animation without her. Hell, he couldn't call it "living" at all. He'd spent his time chasing leads about her all over the globe, incapable of "respecting her privacy" the way her father had demanded. "I've searched everywhere for you."

He wanted answers about where she'd been. If she'd been kidnapped or if she'd left him of her own free will. His private investigators had spent endless hours chasing down fake leads for her whereabouts—it was as if she'd wanted to purposely disappear, or someone had spent significant time making it look that way.

He still had her wedding rings that she'd left behind.

But he remembered reading somewhere that chasing

memories wasn't good for an amnesia victim. And didn't the fact that she was suffering from amnesia suggest she'd been through a trauma already? The need to protect her—to make sure nothing else hurt her—overrode everything else. He needed to keep her safe and get her healthy.

And, selfishly, he couldn't help but see her return as a second chance.

If she'd left him, she didn't remember.

Once she was well and whole again, Damon had a chance to rewrite history. To show her they could be good together again.

To win her back.

"I don't know where I've been. My memories should come back in time." She pulled a hand from her sweater pocket and smoothed aside the wave of hair that brushed her cheek. For a moment, he could see the old Caroline in the gesture. The vibrant, flirtatious woman who had captivated him the moment she strode into his office, demanding a position on his team. "But until they do, I'm not sure where to go. I've been at a shelter the last two nights."

The idea appalled him. How long had they been in the same state while he'd been lost in alternating bouts of grief and bitterness, not knowing what had happened to her?

"You were right to come home." He stepped closer, careful to give her space but needing to touch her.

She flinched and backed up a step, reminding him

that they might be married but they were still essentially strangers in her mind.

She just needed time. Something he was more than happy to give her since he was determined to help her remember how happy they'd been together before that one stupid argument. And, hell, if she *hadn't* been happy, he'd make her remember something better than that.

"You belong here, Caroline," he assured her. "Always."

# Two

To keep her guilty conscience at bay, Caroline sank deeper into the thick cushions of the hanging daybed on the second-floor patio and thought about her son—her whole reason for lying her way into Damon's home.

Lucas was safe with her sister, Victoria, in a carriage house Caroline had rented for them nearby. She'd paid in cash and used a fake name to ensure their father wouldn't find them. She'd timed their trip to coincide with his business visit to Singapore, but she doubted their absence had remained a secret past the first forty-eight hours, which meant he could be learning about their defection anytime now. Would he guess that Caroline had run straight to Damon in Los Altos

Hills? Would he be worried about their safety and send the police?

She had no idea, but she knew Lucas and Victoria would be safer in the carriage house than with her. Victoria swore that their father had purposely tried to keep her from seeing Caroline while she was recovering from her ordeal. Her version of events since Caroline's return—so different from her father's—had been the impetus to see Damon for herself. To find out if he loved her or if he'd only married her for expediency's sake.

Still, she found it difficult to accept that her father coveted Transparent so badly that he would use her as a pawn. She'd been kidnapped, after all. How could Damon have kept that a secret from her family? Her father would have reported her missing if he'd known, but he said that her bills—cell phone, car payments, the mortgage on a small apartment she maintained in Manhattan—were being paid consistently, even during the times when she'd been a captive.

How was that possible? Someone was lying to her, or else she really was going crazy.

Caroline stared into the leaping flames in the stone fireplace and tried to relax before Damon returned. He'd started the blaze to ward off the late afternoon chill as the sun set over San Francisco Bay in the distance. The view was beautiful and the patio heater nearby sent bonus warmth her way. As if the blankets she burrowed under weren't enough. Damon had dragged half the linen closet outdoors when she professed a desire to sit on the patio, extending her the courtesy he might give an invalid.

Which made sense, considering he thought she was suffering from amnesia. And she still did suffer from it, of course. Just not to the degree she pretended.

While she waited for him to return with their dinner, she closed her eyes and reminded herself this was absolutely necessary. She couldn't think of any other way to find out if he had only wed her for material gain, or if he'd genuinely cared for her. And she refused to introduce him to Lucas until she knew for sure. For now, all she knew for certain was that her husband hadn't come for her when she'd been kidnapped. Her captors said he didn't pay the ransom and didn't want her back. While she had no reason to trust them whatsoever, her father's version of events supported this.

He'd sworn he hadn't known she was missing until that fisherman discovered her. But something didn't add up, and she knew her father would lie to further his own ends—of course he would. He hadn't even breathed Damon's name in his house when she'd still been confused about her ordeal and couldn't remember who the father of her child was. How could her dad do that? He'd always been manipulative, relentlessly steering Caroline in the direction he wanted. But she'd drawn the line at allowing him to tell her who she could—and could not—marry.

She would learn all she could in the next two days, and then she would tell Damon the truth. Two days was her limit for being apart from Lucas. But if there was a chance she and Damon could have a future together, she would introduce him to Lucas personally and maybe they could be a family. If it turned out that Damon had never loved her and married her for self-serving purposes?

She would hire a lawyer and sue for full custody through formal channels. She had her own money, accounts solely in her name. She'd changed all the passwords on them last week after discovering someone might have accessed them to pay her bills while she'd been held captive. If necessary, she would hire a financial investigator to help her track what happened there. But her balances were still healthy from her years of nonstop work before she'd met Damon. And right now, she cared far more about her personal affairs than her bottom line.

"Caroline?" Damon asked quietly from the opposite end of the patio, a tray of food in his hands. He must have come up the outdoor stairs; she'd been so caught up in her thoughts, she hadn't heard. She would need to be more careful, more on guard in the future.

He waited there now, balancing the heavy, domed silver platter. With his dark brown hair and deep blue eyes, her husband shared the features of his equally handsome brothers she'd met at their wedding. Damon was slightly taller than Jager and Gabe, though, his six-foot-three frame well-proportioned. And whereas his younger brother, Gabe, possessed an easygoing nature that made him quick to smile, Damon was serious, often pensive and intense. More like his driven older brother, Jager, who managed the brothers' businesses while Damon and Gabe both tended to follow their passions. Damon had always been deeply passionate about his work, he could lose track of the hours spent on business, and he told her once that she was the only woman who'd ever intrigued him enough to get him to spend time away from his company.

He'd had the same effect on her, enticing her out of her office to savor a sunny day or breathe in a cool breeze off the Santa Cruz Mountains.

"Yes?" She straightened from her slouch, propping herself higher on the back pillows so they could share the daybed like a sofa.

A spark arced and popped from the stone fireplace.

"Just checking to make sure you hadn't fallen asleep." He headed her way with the tray, settling it on the low tile table nearby. He'd changed from his earlier cargos and tee to a lightweight black wool sweater and gray trousers. The winds off the bay were chilly now that the sun had gone down. "Are you sure you'll be warm enough out here?" He checked the setting on the patio heater and held his broad palms out to test the temperature. "We can take dinner inside, if you prefer."

"This is perfect, actually." She remembered those early days of recovering her memory when she had grounded herself in the everyday, simple things to anchor her. Enjoying the feel of a warm bath. Stroking the furry back of her sister's cat, Socrates. "I saw a physician about the amnesia in Mexico and she said that surrounding myself with the familiar will help me to recover my memories." Caroline smoothed a hand over the cashmere blanket that Damon had given her earlier, her heart picking up pace as she prepared to dig for information. "I'll bet I spent a lot of time on this swing."

Damon settled on the edge of the cushion beside her, the warmth of his sudden nearness making her senses come alive. She'd forgotten the way he smelled—the musk and spice of his aftershave that sent a flood of pleasurable memories to her brain. Of shared kisses. Incredible sex. Orgasms. Curling into his side afterward and having him stroke her back until she fell asleep.

Her body tingled at just the thoughts.

"None." His blunt response was so at odds with everything she was feeling—the word as stark as his expression. "This house was still being built while we were on our honeymoon in Florence and the Tuscan countryside. We never spent any time here."

She held her breath, waiting for him to say something about the day she'd been abducted. The only day she'd ever stepped inside the completed house. The events of that afternoon were still fuzzy in her mind. Her father had insisted she was planning to leave Damon that day, but she couldn't remember why.

When he continued, however, his attention had returned to the tray of food. "I've only been in town for a few days myself, so I'm afraid the meal offerings aren't as extensive as I would have hoped for your return." He tugged off the silver dome and set it on the stone patio, revealing two empty plates and a cold cut platter. "I called for a grocery delivery and a catered meal for later, but for now, this is the complete contents of the refrigerator."

"The turkey looks good." She leaned forward to make half a sandwich for herself, but Damon politely waved her away.

"Let me." He cut open a small roll and stabbed two slices of meat with the knife. "For months, I would have given anything for the chance to do something for you. See you. Touch you. Bring you dinner."

She swallowed back the knot of emotions his words tangled inside her. What she wouldn't have given to have him there when she'd been scared and alone on that island in Mexico, too ill from her pregnancy to even walk outside and look for a neighboring village.

"What did you think happened to me?" She couldn't help the rasp of her voice that betrayed the pain she kept hidden inside. Clearing her throat, she tried again. "I mean, as I told you, there is nothing about me being missing online."

It was as though she'd simply ceased to exist after their wedding.

He set down the plate with her sandwich on the coffee table before settling his hand on her knee through the blanket. It was the first time he'd touched her since she arrived and it affected her as much as she had feared it might.

"Are you sure you want to talk about this now? So soon after arriving?" He caressed her knee with his thumb through the thick layers of cashmere and wool, the intimacy seeming so easy and natural for him.

As if he truly cared about her.

"I have driven myself crazy trying to piece together the past on my own. I'm hoping you'll help me fill in some of the blanks in a way that will be less stressful."

His blue eyes locked on hers in the firelight, searching.

Could he read her better than she realized? Did he have any inkling that she might not be telling him the whole truth? Never in her life had she felt so unsure of herself as she had these last few months. She used to be so steady and self-assured. Now, everything her father had told her about her past contradicted what she had believed about it.

"I definitely don't want to add to the stress of remembering." Damon returned to the tray and finished making her turkey sandwich, which he passed over before pouring her a drink—water with a twist of lemon. "I did a quick scan online about amnesia recovery while the housekeeper put together the meal, and it said that the senses can sometimes trigger memories more easily. Hearing a song or smelling something familiar can help, like your physician said."

Thinking about the flood of memories from the scent

of his aftershave, Caroline would say the doctor had been spot on.

"If I never lived here, maybe there's nothing to be gained by me staying here." She had allotted two days to solving the mystery of Damon. She couldn't afford to waste time. "Is there somewhere else that might be more meaningful?"

Nibbling on her sandwich, she watched him make another for himself, the muscles in his forearm shifting and flexing as he reached for cheese slices and fresh tomato. She'd fallen for him hard and fast the first time—getting engaged after knowing him for only six weeks and marrying him a month after that. She needed to be more cautious now, to learn all she could about him.

"You lived in a hotel when you first came to town to research Transparent. I had a smaller house close to the company in Mountain View." He leaned back against the cushions lining the daybed swing, keeping a foot on the patio floor to anchor them.

Caroline was grateful both for the darkness and Damon's focus on keeping the daybed from rocking, which took his attention away from her while her face flamed with memories of time spent at his place. How many nights had she languished in his bed there before their wedding? They'd made love in virtually every room. Also, the sauna. The pool house…

She didn't dare ask him about that home. Her voice might betray her.

"Did we have dates anywhere significant? Special?"

She frowned, trying to remember how it felt to have no frame of reference for conversations about the past. When her amnesia had been at its worst, she'd asked questions constantly. "Or maybe we should visit the business, if that's how we met."

Would seeing her office help? They'd worked in the same building.

But she needed to be careful. Damon was a very smart man. Brilliant, even. She'd been fascinated by his mind and his innovative ideas for Transparent even before they'd met. One misstep in her ruse could ruin her cover story for being here.

"We went hiking in the Santa Cruz Mountains once." He studied her with a clear blue gaze that missed nothing. "And you were fixated on the Winchester Mystery House for a while. We had picnics in the gardens while you kept an eye out for ghosts."

His unexpected choice of memories touched her. Those outings were such brief pockets of time they'd spent together compared to the long hours they'd invested in his business and, later, trying to deal with her father.

Her driven, focused father would have hated that she'd gone ghost-hunting. Did he know she'd ever done something like that?

"Do you remember?" Damon asked suddenly, making her realize she'd been quiet a beat too long, thinking about how thoroughly her father had schooled her to think like him, to fill her days with work the way he did.

"No." She shook her head quickly, returning her gaze to her plate. "I'm just surprised to imagine myself ghost-watching. It hardly sounds like the hobby of a businesswoman."

She'd been a different person with Damon, though. Their courtship had been a revelation. It hadn't just been about love. It had been about play. Fun. Laughter.

Things she hadn't really taken the time to savor in a life full of goals set ever higher ever since childhood, from violin recitals to debate team championships to achieving perfect test scores. Then, after graduating from college, it had been about obtaining a lucrative position in a New York financial firm before joining her father's company. Her father had trained her to focus on work relentlessly, while Damon wasn't afraid to enjoy himself.

"I think you liked the diversion of something whimsical after the stress of long days at the office." He took a bite of his sandwich and seemed to reconsider the answer. "Then again, maybe you were just trying to give *me* a diversion after the long days at the office. We never did see any ghosts."

And his sense of whimsy had faded, she recalled, toward the end of their honeymoon when her father had urged her to come to London to help him with a takeover of a UK company. She'd been excited for the chance to end the standoff with him. Damon had been stunned she would even consider it. In the end, she'd told him she would head to London anyhow to see a friend and at least meet with her father. It had been an unhappy way to wind up their romantic Italy trip.

But could it have really been the end of their marriage?

"Then let's try again." She still hoped their son could one day see the more lighthearted, loving side of Damon. Provided it ever existed outside her hopeful imagination. "Let's go back to a place with happy memories."

The next day, with Caroline in the passenger seat of his white Land Rover, Damon pulled into the Los Trancos Preserve in the mountains above Palo Alto. The woods were close to the house, easy to access from the home they'd built together.

It seemed like a million years ago now. Their dating. Their marriage. Even her disappearance. Last night, after she went to bed, he had reopened his old investigation notes from those frantic first few months she'd been gone. He'd taken his time reading over everything again, looking for new clues now that he knew she'd been in Mexico. All of the evidence he'd found on her whereabouts had led him to believe she was in Europe. She'd deposited money in her account in London and used an ATM card in Prague, Paris and Venice. Her credit card had been used for a room in a Barcelona hotel, but when his PI had shown her picture around the place, no one on staff recognized her.

Had someone been impersonating her? At the time,

he'd guessed she wanted to disappear and had paid someone well to cover her tracks. Whatever the case, it was as much a mystery as ever. While he was inside the house retrieving food for Caroline, he'd also messaged the PI his half brothers had used to find him when he'd been traveling Europe looking for her on his own. At the time, he had ditched his cell phone so as not to be distracted with work calls or requests from his family to return home. He'd bought a burner and focused on following Caroline's trail, but he'd come up empty handed.

Bentley, the investigator who had located Damon when Jager and Gabe got fed up with his disappearing act, was excellent. But unfortunately, he'd been hired by a branch of Damon's family he would rather forget. Damon's father, Liam, had left their mother when they were kids and Damon, Jager, and Gabe had no use for the guy. But recently, their grandfather, Malcolm McNeill, had made it his mission to reunite all of his grandchildren, even the illegitimate branch. Damon might not have much use for all the new blood relatives in his life, and most especially not his father, but he could appreciate the value of a good PI. Maybe Bentley would figure out what a whole team of investigators had failed to the first time around.

Just what the hell had happened to his wife?

Talking about the good times with her last night had felt surreal, like the experiences had happened to someone else. He'd been trying so damn hard to forget her, and now? She'd forgotten all about him instead.

If that meant she forgot all about her bastard of a

father, Damon didn't mind the sacrifice one bit. He hoped the subject of Stephan Degraff wouldn't surface between them today since Damon knew he wouldn't be able to scrounge a single positive thing to say about the guy who was still fighting to take control of Transparent. Her father was on a mission to turn the rest of the investors against Damon so they could pull in a more experienced CEO to run the company.

Over his dead body.

"Are you sure you feel up to this?" Damon asked Caroline as he switched off the Land Rover. "We could always go for a Sunday drive instead."

She was as beautiful as ever, but her pale skin and thinner frame made her seem frailer somehow. Or maybe it was simply because he knew she'd suffered a trauma that had given her amnesia. He didn't want her to exhaust herself. He'd suggested she call a doctor first thing this morning, wanting to know what a professional had to say about her condition, but she'd been adamant she was well enough. When he hadn't backed down, she'd conceded to a visit tomorrow if they could have one day together first.

He'd been hard pressed to argue. He was having a tough time just letting her out of his sight. Tomorrow would be soon enough.

"I'll be fine." She gave him a smile that threw caution to the wind. He remembered it from when they'd climbed the bell tower in Florence and she'd challenged him to see who could scale the four-hundred-some steps faster. "The fresh air and exercise will be good for me."

He still wanted to wrap her in cotton and keep watch over her for days, but he nodded.

Leaving the picnic basket in the back, he locked his door before stalking around to her side and helping her down. He only touched her briefly, putting his hand on her forearm to steady her while she hopped out, but it reminded him how long it had been since he'd touched a woman. Touched her. Even when he'd thought she was never coming back, he hadn't consoled himself with someone else. In his mind, he'd still been married.

He watched Caroline take in the sights, her head turning as she studied the oak woodland and grassy knolls, the combination of forest and rolling hills scented with bay leaves and the cool, damp earth. The sun shone warmly enough for a southern California winter day, but little light penetrated the thickest patches of trees nearby.

Dressed in a dark blue running suit and a pink tee she'd found in her closet, she started toward the closest hiking trail, her new white sneakers fast on the well-worn path.

"Ready?" Her ponytail swung around her shoulder as she turned back to see him.

"Which way looks good?" he asked, curious if she had even a subconscious memory of the place.

"It seems sunniest in that direction." She pointed to-ward the grassier path heading south.

He followed her, discreetly lifting branches out of her way when low boughs seemed too close to head height. For the most part, however, the trail was wide open and the preserve was quiet save for an older man taking his Dalmatian for a walk.

When they reached a high spot with a view of the Bay, Caroline dropped down to a flat rock and zipped her jacket up midway. Damon sat beside her, admiring the view from the peak, and all the time debating if he should ask her more about her ordeal or if he should focus on making new, happier memories. Before he could decide, she turned dark brown eyes his way.

"You said you searched everywhere for me." Her voice was quiet. Serious. "Why didn't you report me missing?"

The wind whistled through the tree branches overhead, a lonely sound that echoed through him.

Yesterday, when they'd touched on this subject, he'd been too stunned by the realization that she didn't remember him to focus on the question. Now, he heard the hurt in her voice. The doubts underlying the question. She had hesitated to come back to him, thinking he might have "moved on."

Which gave him no choice but to bring up her father.

He ground his teeth at the very thought of the man.

"Your father showed the police proof you'd been in touch with him. He said you'd left the marriage of your own volition and said I should respect your privacy." He studied her expression, trying to interpret what she might be feeling at that news. "Do you remember much about him?"

"No. I've made progress since those first days where I didn't recognize my own name. I can visualize my family, as well as college and the jobs I had after I graduated. But I don't really remember anything about why I came out to Los Altos Hills. The last apartment I can recall clearly was in New York City." She drew her knees up to her chest and wrapped her arms around them. "I can remember that I worked for my father, and I have a few memories of my childhood, but not much about him personally."

Just his luck, she hadn't wiped out all memory of Stephan Degraff. Just of Damon.

"Then you might recall your close relationship with your father," he ventured carefully. "How often the two of you spoke." Stephan Degraff counted on Caroline's business advice for his investments, calling on her anytime day or night if he had a question. The guy was relentless. Manipulative. And then, a disturbing thought occurred to Damon. "I'm surprised you didn't go to him first if you didn't recollect anything about me."

"I—" She hesitated, a mixture of emotions evident in her eyes. Guilt. Worry.

"It doesn't matter." He covered her knee with one hand, not wishing to upset her. "I'm glad you came here."

"But my father told the police that I left you? Was it you who called the police?"

"You texted me when your plane landed after you returned here from London." He wasn't going to mention the argument they'd had about the UK trip. "It didn't make sense to me that you would contact me then, only to pack up and leave me."

"Of course not." She shook her head, ponytail swinging. "Unless we'd been unhappy?"

"Right after the honeymoon?" He removed his hand from her knee to withdraw his phone and tapped open the gallery of images he'd saved. "Scroll through a few of those and see if they look like pictures of unhappy people."

She shifted positions, lowering her knees to glance over the photos of them on the Ponte Vecchio, seated at their favorite café for morning espressos, in front of the Uffizi Gallery, at the top of that bell tower they'd climbed. Most of the images were of her smiling and him kissing her cheek, but in a few of them, you could see them both grinning. Wildly in love.

Or so he thought.

"My God." Her finger swiped faster, sending pictures spinning off the screen, one after another. "Did you show these to the police? To my father? What did they say?"

Her voice quavered. Her whole body seemed to tremble. *Damn it.*

"I'm sorry." He wrapped an arm around her shoulders and gently slid the phone from her hands. "I didn't mean to upset you. We'll figure it all out, okay? Just relax."

She shook like a leaf. He couldn't understand what, precisely, had her so troubled. But he didn't want to rile her more.

"This is too important for me to relax." Edging away from his touch, she shot to her feet and paced around the small lookout spot. "Would you be able to put me in touch with the officers you spoke to? The police who supposedly talked to my dad?"

"Supposedly?" Getting to his feet, he frowned. Defensive. "You don't believe me?"

She tipped her head to one side. Thinking. "I've invested a lot of time struggling to piece together the past. I don't want to worry that the perspectives I'm hearing are biased. I'd like to know what a neutral party has to say."

"Of course." He reached for her again, needing to offer some kind of comfort when she was clearly rattled. "Caroline, it's not good for you to be so agitated. Let's think about something else. Something happier."

"Why would you believe I left of my own free will if we were so happy?" With her lips pursed and her eyebrows scrunched in confusion, she stared up at him waiting for answers he didn't have.

Okay. Answers he didn't want to share.

"Every couple argues. When your father said you'd been contacting him regularly, I assumed I must have missed something, but you'd be home soon." He didn't want to delve into this now. Not when his whole purpose today had been to relive good times.

"And when months went by?" She peered up at him, frustration simmering in her clear brown eyes.

"I took solace from the knowledge that you loved me once and you'd love me again." He dropped his palms on her shoulders, drawing her closer. Wanting her to feel the connection that still stirred inside him every time she was near. "I knew what we shared wouldn't just disappear. I hired private investigators to find you myself."

He could feel her swift intake of breath. A mixture of wariness and some warmer, answering emotion flared in her eyes, but she didn't move away.

The wind stirred the leaves at their feet and whirled around them. To Damon, it felt like it was drawing them closer.

"I'd like to show you what I mean." He teased a touch along her jaw, testing the softness of her creamy skin, breathing in the faint scent of roses.

He wanted to take his time, to soak in the feel of her, the warmth.

If she remembered nothing else, she had to remember this.

Slowly, he grazed his lips along hers, the barest brush of mouths. Of breath. He tipped his forehead to hers, standing still, waiting.

When her fingers curled into his shoulders, her nails softly pressing through his sweater and tee, Damon's blood surged in a heated rush. He ground his teeth against the bolt of hunger and forced himself to step back. He simply took her hands in his and caressed and kissed them.

"That proves passion is still there," she said finally, her voice expressing the same hunger he felt. Yet she backed up another step and slid her hands away from his, tucking them into her pockets. "But what about love?"

# Three

Late that night, safe in the master suite that Damon had wanted her to use during her stay, Caroline called her sister on a burner phone to check on Lucas.

Her Mexican captivity had been frightening and lonely, but the experience had taught her about making herself difficult to find. The men who'd held her went through cheap, pay-by-the-minute phones like candy, opening new packages of them every week. They were perfect for contacting their colleagues and not leaving a trace. When Caroline left Vancouver with her son and her sister three days ago, she'd purchased similar devices at a few different places along the way, driving almost to Montana to cross the border discreetly.

Illegally.

But since they were US citizens anyhow, she didn't feel as guilty about that as she did about deceiving Damon. Assuming, of course, that he really did love her. Even before the toe-curling kiss he'd given her on the hiking trail, those honeymoon photos he'd shown her had gotten to her. Could that kind of happiness be faked? She knew she'd been in love with him. But the pictures had her almost believing he sincerely felt the same way for her.

Almost. And she needed to be absolutely certain.

Because if Damon was being forthright about what they'd shared and about her father's role in not reporting her missing—that meant her dad was guilty of... She didn't even want to think about it. If that was the case, her father had far more to answer for than simply withholding the truth about her husband.

Earlier in the evening, she'd attempted to phone the two police officers Damon had spoken to, but neither was on duty. Surely Damon had to feel confident they would back up his story if he provided their names so readily?

Her sister answered the phone on the third ring, sounding flustered or maybe scared. "Caroline? Are you okay?"

Victoria's worry fueled her own. Caroline sat up straighter.

"I'm fine. Are you safe? Is Lucas okay?"

She could hear Victoria huff out a breath on the other

end, relaxing. In the background, the laugh track from an old sitcom added an odd note to their tense greeting.

"We're good. He's fast asleep in the other room and I have the baby monitor right next to me so I can hear if he so much as sighs."

A pang of longing stabbed Caroline in the chest. She wished she were holding her infant son right now, the warmth of his small body comforting her and giving her strength after this stress-filled day.

"I miss him so much. Thank you for taking care of him." She drew a steadying breath herself, padding over to the California king–size bed to slip between the luxurious sheets. She propped herself on down pillows stacked against the leather bolster. The room's color scheme of tans and creams was so neutral it felt like an old sepia-toned photograph. "Have you seen anyone? Heard anything?"

They'd both been worried their father would have them followed. Or he'd cut short the Singapore trip to come after them himself. It didn't matter that they'd crossed the border in secret; Stephan Degraff would probably guess Caroline's ultimate destination. Her father knew she was upset that he'd withheld Damon's name from her when she'd been confused and suffering from amnesia.

At the time, her sister had been doing a semester abroad program for her degree and hadn't been aware of what was happening. Victoria had some flexibility in her schedule this semester to work on her master's thesis, but she was due back at Stanford by the end of the month.

"It's been quiet. I haven't left the carriage house and I've kept the blinds drawn, like we talked about. I've got enough diapers and formula for a whole week, I think."

"I'll be back long before then." She briefly relayed to Victoria what she'd learned from Damon, ending with the news that an officer from the Santa Clara County Sheriff's Department was supposed to return her call in the morning.

After a long silence, Victoria let out a low whistle. "My God, Caro, I don't even know what to say." She swore softly. "Because if your husband is telling the truth, that means Dad is—"

"Dangerous?" She barely breathed the word, not wanting to believe it herself.

When her sister scoffed, Caroline shifted against the pillows, flipping the cream-colored sheet up higher against her red floral nightshirt.

"Dad might be controlling," Victoria mused aloud, the laugh track still rolling from the television in the background. "Hell-bent on winning, even, but that doesn't make him dangerous."

Right. This was the father who'd pushed them on the swing when they were girls and used it as a fun physics lesson. The same dad who took them camping and taught them how to tell which plants were poisonous. He might have had high expectations for his daughters, but Caroline had never had reason to doubt his love.

"How could he not have been worried if Damon told him he thought I was kidnapped?" She felt like she was missing pieces of a bigger puzzle. "Why wouldn't he have at least looked into the possibility? Was he that angry with me that I married someone he didn't approve of?" She thought back on the last few months in her father's house. At first, she'd been ill. But as she gained strength and her memories began returning, she'd told him she'd been abducted. "Furthermore, why didn't he call the police when I told him what I remembered about the men who held me against my will?"

"But Damon said Dad told the cops you'd been in contact with him shortly after you were taken," Victoria said carefully. "Maybe that's true and you still have gaps in your memory from the drugs?"

"I do have gaps in my memory. I know that." Frustration simmered, but how could she expect other people to believe her version of past events when she had so many doubts of her own? "But I didn't imagine that house in Mexico or the rotating staff of guards who stood watch every day for months."

A shiver chilled her skin and she burrowed deeper in the covers, tugging the khaki-colored duvet up over the sheet. She reached a hand out of the blankets long enough to tap the remote for the gas fireplace. The flames leaped higher inside the pale-river-stone hearth. The house was quiet and she wondered if Damon was still awake. He'd kept things light between them after their kiss, his behavior toward her solicitous, polite…

caring, even. But he'd seemed determined not to revisit conversation topics that could "agitate" her and he'd reminded her over dinner that she'd promised to see a doctor tomorrow.

For the amnesia she didn't really have. The last holes in her memory now were drug-induced and, her doctor said, might never return.

"Okay." Victoria turned down the television on her end of the call. "But what if the gaps in your memory are bigger than you realize? What if you were a captive for weeks and not months? Isn't there a chance Dad could be telling the truth about having contact with you at first? Maybe you just don't remember that you left Damon—like Dad said—because it was too upsetting."

Her chest constricted. She wasn't sure if she resisted the idea because she still cared about her husband, or because she wanted her son to have a relationship with his father. Or both.

"Why wouldn't I have told you if I left my husband?" Caroline asked, tracing the buttons on the fireplace remote with her thumbnail.

Victoria was her closest confidante and had been since they lost their mother to an overdose of prescription opioids five years ago. Actually, she'd been closer to Victoria since well before that, as their mother had struggled with depression for years before her death. Caroline and Damon had that loss in common; his had died when he was young. At least she'd been close with her father. Damon's dad had stopped visiting his illegitimate sons before Damon was a teen, choosing to be a father to his offspring by his legal wife rather than Damon and his brothers.

"Just guessing, but I was buried in coursework that semester, so maybe you held off because of that." She seemed to hesitate and for a moment Caroline heard nothing but the soft hiss of the flames in the fireplace before Victoria continued. "Or maybe you were keeping me out of it since Dad asked you to keep your distance from me when you chose to marry his business enemy."

It was all speculation of course, since Victoria couldn't know Caroline's reasons any better than Caroline did. A wave of fatigue hit her.

"But I remember someone entering the house. And it wasn't Damon." She had to have been kidnapped. She remembered being frightened that day.

"You were drugged," Victoria said softly. "There's a reason they give benzodiazepines to patients to forget about surgery. It makes things fuzzy and confusing. Time bends. That's not your fault, Caroline."

Right. Her physician had said the same thing. But that didn't make it any less scary or infuriating.

Before she could say as much, however, she heard a baby's cry on the other end of the call. She sat up straight in bed, poised to help before reminding herself that she wasn't in the same house as Lucas.

"Guess it's time for the midnight bottle." The crying quieted for a moment; Victoria must have turned down the volume on the baby monitor. "I'd better go."

"Okay. Wish I was there." Caroline wanted her baby with her. Always.

She hated that she had to deceive people—her father and her husband, too—just to find out who was telling her the truth.

"Soon. Be safe, Caro. And good luck." Victoria disconnected, leaving Caroline feeling more alone than ever.

Tomorrow, she'd have to find a way to divert Damon from her doctor's appointment. She would go in person to the police station if she didn't hear from the officers first thing in the morning. Her future was riding on what they had to say. Because once she found out if Damon had been telling her truth, she would confront him with her own: that although she couldn't remember if she'd left him or not, she knew without a doubt she'd been held against her will for some of the time.

Damon had been the man she'd missed then, the one person she'd yearned to see. No drugs could make her forget how much she'd loved him once. Too bad she was no closer to knowing if he'd felt the same about her. Worse, she feared that even if he had returned those feelings at one time, she might have destroyed that love forever by keeping their child a secret.

"I've got a simple solution for all your problems, brother," Damon's younger brother told him in their Skype call at dawn.

Well, dawn West Coast time. Where Gabe sat, on

the back patio of the Birdsong Hotel near the McNeill family compound in Martinique, it was already late morning. Exotic birds chirped in the palms swaying behind him, the whole image like an eighties pop-art painting full of pinks and turquoise.

"My missing bride finally returns home and doesn't remember me. Her investor father wants to kick me out of my own company. I found a glitch in the new software we're about to launch. And our older brother is happy just to sell off everything and get out of Dodge so he can spend time with his new wife." Damon sat in the breakfast nook off the kitchen, one of the few rooms in the gargantuan house that didn't echo when he had a phone conversation. Also, he'd chosen this spot since it was close to the stairs from the master suite, and he needed to stick near Caroline. "Now, explain to me how you could possibly have a solution to all those problems."

Gabe had surprised him with the call this morning after Damon texted him the night before, asking for his opinion on the potential sale of Transparent. Their older brother, Jager, wanted the sale to happen so they could start over and get out from under the pressure of investors who wanted to control the direction of the company.

Namely, Stephan Degraff.

Damon couldn't let go yet. He was grateful to Jager for leading the company while Damon had searched for Caroline. But now he was ready to return his focus to the technology he'd developed. Technology he believed in. He wasn't selling. And he wasn't allowing Stephan Degraff to unseat him from the board, either.

"Go to New York," Gabe informed him simply, spreading his arms wide as he rocked back in a purple-painted lounge chair, as if the answer was obvious. "Call on the new family relations and see if the McNeills will put their legendary money where the old man's mouth is. Granddad says he wants us to be part of the family. Let him dust off the wallet and buy out Degraff to prove it."

"Spoken like the baby of the family." Damon leaned back against the leather banquette cushion and toasted Gabe with a mug of black coffee. "It doesn't gall you even a little to go begging for a handout?"

"Who's begging? Degraff would sell out his own kid to take over Transparent and the dude is worth a fortune. Clearly there is capital to be gained from your software idea." Gabe shrugged, his sunglasses glinting with the reflected noontime glare. "Although, to be honest, I only invested because we're related."

"Generous to a fault, you are." Damon shook his head, content to let Gabe ramble on about his assessment of "Granddad" following a recent phone call. But Damon's thoughts lingered on something else his brother had said.

How much would Stephan Degraff "sell out" Caroline to obtain control of Transparent? What lengths would he go to?

A year ago, Damon had told himself that it didn't matter what Stephan did because Damon's love for Caroline surpassed everything else. But what if Stephan hadn't just sent Caroline to Transparent for business reasons—to be Damon's entrepreneur in residence? What if Caroline had come to get close to Damon personally, as well?

The idea was ridiculous. She was a beautiful, brilliant woman. She would have never married him solely because her father wanted to spy on Damon's company. But the fact that she'd disappeared right after the honeymoon, coupled with the fact that she'd returned now, claiming to have no memory of the marriage, right at a sensitive time of transition for the business…

Across the kitchen, he saw the door of the master bedroom open silently. He closed his laptop with no warning to Gabe, not wanting Caroline to overhear the discussion. Damon watched her as she stepped onto the bamboo floor, her shoes in her hand, as if she wanted to make as little sound as possible. She was fully dressed in fresh clothes she must have found in the closet. A cranberry-colored purse was slung over the shoulder of a shawl sweater that swung around her knees. Her gaze was on the door.

Leaving?

"Good morning."

He startled her so badly she dropped the shoes she'd been carrying, brown leather boots that clunked heavily to the floor. Damn it. How had he let his brother's comment twist him around to think the worst of their relationship? He knew Caroline better than that. Didn't he?

Shoving to his feet, he was across the room and at her side. Picking up her shoes and setting them neatly by the kitchen island, he reached to steady her arm.

"I'm sorry, Caroline." He smoothed a touch along her shoulder, remembering the feel of her lips against his the day before. "I should have given you a warning."

"No need." She waved off the apology, her high ponytail brushing her shoulder when she moved away. "You live here. I'm the newcomer." She tipped the cell phone in her hand to show him. "I'm on hold with the local police department. I'm trying to speak to the officers you mentioned yesterday."

"I thought they were going to call you when they went on duty?" He had been with her when they'd left a message at the station the day before.

"Shift change is at seven a.m. I thought I'd try to reach them before they head out for the day." Her attention shifted to the call and she tucked the phone against her cheek. "Yes, I'm here. I'm holding for Officer Downey."

Damon watched her pace the kitchen, her outfit a swirl of rich colors reflected in stainless steel appliances. She must have been transferred to the officer she wanted because she gave her name and the details of why she was calling, checking notes that she pulled from her purse to read him approximate dates Damon had given her yesterday.

Having his story checked was a strange sensation. Long before he'd dreamed up the idea for Transparent, he'd been a successful businessman. In Martinique, where he and his brothers owned a marina and a historic plantation home available for private parties and corporate retreats, he had a reputation for being a fair employer and a generous contributor to local causes. In Silicon Valley, he was a man people listened to. He filled lecture halls when he spoke at prestigious universities about digital progress.

But the woman he'd given his heart to had to verify his story with the police. Was that normal for amnesia sufferers? He added it to the list of things to ask the specialist, who'd made time to see her today when he called in a favor from a friend.

For now, he distracted himself by making a fresh pot of coffee for Caroline while she quizzed the cop on the other end of the phone.

"Thank you so much," she finally said, her brown eyes darting Damon's way. "I appreciate knowing more about what my father said." She seemed to hesitate as she listened to the officer. She shook her head even though he couldn't see her. "No," she finally said. "Not yet. But I will contact you as soon as I'm ready to come in to give a statement."

Caroline thumbed the off button and tucked her phone in her bag. Was it his imagination or did she take her time? The suspense was killing him.

"You need to give a statement?" he asked after a moment.

She slid the purse strap off her shoulder and laid the

bag on the gray granite counter of the island. Licking her lips, she eyed him warily, ignoring the coffee mug he'd set out for her.

"I suffered amnesia, Damon." Her chin was tilted, her posture defensive. "But I've recovered more memories than I led you to believe when I showed up here two days ago."

That…was not what he'd expected.

Two days ago, he'd been sure she'd only come to see him to obtain a divorce. He braced himself for that news now, his whole body tensing.

"Why would you do that? Mislead me into thinking you didn't remember what happened between us?" He hated that he hadn't been a better husband. That he'd allowed her father to come between them when he'd known from the start that Stephan Degraff only wanted to get his hands on Transparent.

He couldn't believe that Caroline had been a part of her father's plan to usurp him all along. Refused to believe it.

"I needed to know why you didn't report me missing." The hurt in her eyes seemed real enough. "It didn't make any sense. Besides, my father told me—"

"Your father?" His worse fears were confirmed. She'd been talking to that bastard all along.

Cold filled the hollow pit in his gut.

"He found me in Mexico. Helped me to locate a doctor to treat my amnesia—"

"When?" Damon regretted the harshness of his tone,

but it was as though his heart had been ripped right out of his chest. Forcing his voice lower, he took a steadying breath. "Exactly how long have you and your father been playing me, Caroline? For two days? Or from the very beginning?"

# Four

Caroline closed her eyes for a moment, giving herself a chance to think about her child. If Damon had truly loved her at one time, she owed it to Lucas to find out. Those photos from the honeymoon had filled her dreams the night before, stirring the slimmest hope that she and Damon could find some kind of happiness again.

Assuming the connection hadn't been faked the first time.

She ached for the deep love she'd seen in those photos. But as she opened her eyes to meet Damon's frosty blue glare, she wondered if she could ever find it again. He rose from the dining table in the breakfast nook, leaving his phone and laptop abandoned on the sleek hardwood surface as he stalked toward her. He stood on the opposite end of the island from her, almost as if that was as close as he could bear to be.

"My father doesn't even know I'm here," she told him when she felt steady enough to respond to his accusation. She was walking a thin line here, being truthful about her father, but being dishonest about her amnesia and not sharing about the baby. "I've been struggling to remember what happened this past year and I have reason to believe Dad was thwarting my efforts more than helping them."

Damon's head tipped back, the subtlest evidence that her words hit him like a blow. "So you don't deny it? You ran to your father when you left me?"

"I was abducted from this house ten and a half months ago, Damon. I was upstairs in the spare bedroom I planned to make into my office when someone came in." She hadn't set foot in that room on this visit, afraid she would have a panic attack if she recalled what happened next. The day was blurry in her mind, but she recalled suffocating fear. "That's why I need to make a statement to the police. I was kidnapped, and yet the police never believed I was in any danger."

He laid his broad palms on the island's granite countertop. Once upon a time, he'd put his hands on her, as often as possible. Now, he'd rather keep them splayed on cold stone than touch her.

One more hurt among so many others.

"You just spoke to the police, so you know that's not

true. I called them the same day. I came home and when you weren't here—" He stopped himself and shook his head. "It was your father who said you had been in contact with him. He convinced the cops you were fine."

"And that's why I'm going to the police and making a formal statement." She still held the notepaper in her hand with the dates, times and names of law enforcement officials Damon said he'd spoken to about her whereabouts. "Someone came into this house, put a hood over my head and drugged me. I ended up in Mexico and after being captive in various places, I was abandoned in a house on the Baja Peninsula in Mexico. By then, I'd been drugged multiple times, and I could no longer tell what month it was, let alone what day."

She had been so frightened. All the more so when she'd discovered she was pregnant, since her worries were twice as big for the baby she carried. She'd been terrified the drugs were hurting the precious life inside her. Even through the amnesia, fear for her child's health was the one coherent thought she'd retained. She'd asked her father for multiple pediatricians to assess Lucas's health and make sure he was okay.

Damon's hands flexed against the granite. "I'll take you to the police station myself. They said the ransom note was a hoax, but maybe now they'll see things differently."

Could she trust him? She wanted to, which made her all the more cautious. "The guards told me you didn't give them the money." She'd been deflated that day. It had been a turning point in those lonely weeks of captivity. Because even though she knew to be skeptical of what they told her, she believed they would have released her if Damon had given them the exorbitant sum they'd requested.

"They lied to you. I wired the full amount to an overseas account as requested." He slid his hands off the counter and walked slowly toward her in his socks. He still wore the same clothes as the night before, a black tee and cargoes, tipping her off he'd never been to bed. "I would have paid it twice over to get you back, Caroline, but I didn't trust the cops when they said it was a hoax since you had been in touch with your father and you were still paying your bills—the mortgage on your New York apartment, a car payment on the Mercedes, a few things you kept in your own name after the wedding."

"You paid the ransom?" She swallowed hard, her thoughts shifting again as she discovered yet another new piece to the puzzle that kept changing.

Damon stopped a foot away from her, his strong shoulders too enticing in the morning light slanting into the kitchen. How easy it would be to lean on him. To share the burdens and the confusion. To let him sort out the mess that she couldn't figure out no matter how hard she tried.

"I have proof. I kept meticulous records. I hired private investigators to follow leads." His blue eyes bored into hers, and she had the sense that he was seeking holes in her story. After all, he had just accused her of deceiving him with her father's blessing. "The police can have everything my team discovered."

"I'm sure that would help." Her mouth was dry. Had it been a mistake to reveal all of this to him and not to the police first? She'd been so romanced by those damned honeymoon photos that she'd hoped—maybe she could have more trust in Damon than her father.

"Someone laid a very deliberate false trail, Caroline." He spoke slowly, articulating the idea simply and clearly, as if she was as addle-brained as she'd pretended to be when she showed up. "Do you understand what I'm suggesting? Someone spent a great deal of money making it look like you hadn't been abducted."

She understood what he was saying—and whom he was accusing—but she couldn't believe it. "My father would never knowingly subject me to harm, if that's what you're getting at."

"How can you be so sure? You must have your doubts if you left without telling him where you were going. You came here, to me, even knowing that he wouldn't approve." Damon inched closer, just enough to lay a hand on her shoulder. "So if you're not still playing a game with me, you must distrust him."

She traced the pattern in the gray granite countertop, thinking. She needed to tell him about Lucas. The time had come. "After I was kidnapped and drugged, I truly suffered a bout of amnesia. I was ill. I didn't know who to trust."

"You went to your father."

"At the time, I didn't remember you."

Damon studied her, no doubt weighing her words.

"What made you change your mind?" he asked, his hand falling away from her.

She missed his touch, even when they were at odds. Even when she didn't know if she could truly confide in him.

"My father never mentioned you. He didn't say one word about me being married, even though I was confused about— I couldn't remember anything." She had told her father about the pregnancy, but he claimed not to know anything about who she'd been dating before the kidnapping, suggesting the father of her child was a one-night stand. She had been devastated when she learned the truth. That she'd had a husband who would be hurt to have missed out on their child's birth. "But then my sister came to see me. He couldn't keep me isolated forever. She gave me the marriage certificate. I guess my father had a copy in his office."

It hadn't occurred to her to wonder why. She'd had a lot of other worries in her head and in her heart at that time while she struggled to remember her past.

"Victoria told you the truth." Damon nodded, a satisfied gleam in his eyes. "I've never met her, since your dad forbade anyone in your family to attend our wedding." His jaw flexed. "But of course, you remember that now, don't you?"

"Yes. Victoria's revelation was a big help in recovering more of my memories." Caroline paced around the kitchen island, not trusting herself around Damon when she felt this magnetic draw to him. "And the therapist who was helping me with the amnesia suggested I'd been a victim of gaslighting. She didn't openly accuse my father. I think she believed that maybe my captors had been the ones to feed me lies and withhold information." Caroline hadn't wanted to believe she could be susceptible to suggestion and misinformation, but once Victoria revealed the truth, Caroline had to face the reality that her father no longer had her best interests at heart. "And by then, I knew that it was my father who didn't want me to remember you."

"If any other man hurt you this way…" Damon didn't finish the thought.

He didn't need to.

"Damon." A fresh dose of anxiety poured through her. "I came here because I had suspicions about my father, but I also didn't trust my memories where you're concerned. That's why I pretended to have amnesia to a greater degree than I really do. To see what you'd say."

She tried to gauge his reaction, studying his expression. The kitchen was brightly lit now that the sun had risen well above the horizon. Birds chirped in a nest outside the window near the sink, providing an incongruously cheery soundtrack to the most difficult conversation of her life.

"You should have gone straight to the police." His jaw was set, his shoulders tense. "Do you have any reason to believe those kidnappers won't come after you again? My God, Caroline. You took an incredible risk if you believed me capable of such a thing." He speared a hand through his dark hair, ruffling the long layers shaggy for want of a cut. "Sure, now you know it wasn't me. But you could still be in danger from whoever took you."

"I wanted to see you face-to-face, for myself. To come to this house and see how it felt. What else I might remember." She closed the space between them, leaning against the kitchen island where he still stood. "Maybe that was reckless of me. I'm doing the best I can with the unimaginable things that have happened to me. Who could possibly prepare for what I've been through?"

"We need to talk to the cops. Now." He charged toward the door leading to the three-bay garage.

"Damon, wait." She needed to tell him about Lucas before things went any further and they got law enforcement involved. "There's something else you need to know first."

He stopped. Turned. "Whatever it is, the police will surely want to hear it." He picked up his set of keys from a rack of hooks near the door. "I think you'll be telling the whole story a few times today. The trail for those bastards who took you has long gone cold, but the sooner we can get law enforcement after them—"

"Damon." She followed him, pausing just inches from him. "Please. This is important." She took the keys from his hand. Set them on the bare desktop of a built-in workstation near a wall of cookbooks. "There's another reason it took me so long to get back to you."

"And we can sort through all of it after you give your statement to the police."

There was no way to put this but to simply say it. So she did.

"I was pregnant when they kidnapped me." She had wondered more than once what his reaction would have been like if she'd gotten to tell him the news months ago.

For a moment, he was utterly expressionless. "Pregnant?"

"Yes. I—"

"But you said you were drugged. Didn't those bastards know you were pregnant?" A dangerous light entered his eyes. His nostrils flared.

"*I* didn't even know at first." She blinked fast. Took a deep breath. "But he's fine, Damon. I had our son—a perfectly healthy baby boy—six weeks ago."

# Five

The news staggered him.

Damon stared at Caroline, uncomprehending. They had a son. And she'd been lying to him on every level imaginable. The sting of betrayal tainted what should have been the happiest news of his life.

He had a *son*. But the woman he'd loved hadn't trusted him enough to tell him. She'd gone to her lying, conniving father rather than turning to her husband.

"Damon?" Caroline's voice was tentative.

He realized he'd backed up a step. That he'd some-how dropped onto one of the leather bar stools at the kitchen island while the baby bombshell tore away any hope he'd had that he could salvage the love he'd once had for his wife.

"Where is he now? Our son?" The word tripped awkwardly off his tongue.

"Safe. Victoria helped me and Lucas leave my father's house." She blinked rapidly, no doubt hearing the edge in his voice. "I rented them a small house nearby. I made sure it had a security system. We paid cash and she has the doors locked in case my father tries to have us followed."

Damon felt his fury rising. He would decimate Stephan Degraff's business interests. Ruin him financially. And that was just for starters. He would follow Gabe's advice and make peace with the rest of the McNeills—his grandfather and half brothers—to leverage their business influence if that's what it took to bankrupt Caroline's father.

But first, he needed to prevent himself from falling down the emotional rabbit hole after this latest betrayal from his wife. He had a son to think about.

"We must have conceived during the honeymoon. I didn't know I was pregnant for the first two weeks that I was a captive." She licked her lips, speaking quickly as she straightened a white cup hanging from one of the wooden hooks over the coffee bar. "I didn't have a pregnancy test to confirm it, so it was only a guess for a few weeks, but once I started having morning sickness, I knew for sure."

His brain reminded him he had a role to play here. He was a father now. Protector to a vulnerable child and a wife who could still be the target of a kidnapper who hadn't been caught. He would be a better father than his own worthless DNA contributor had been, so when push came to shove, he would do right by his child and Caroline, too. But it was damned hard to know the right words to say when he didn't trust the mother of his baby.

"We'll talk on the way to the police station." He picked up the Land Rover keys again, determined to get a statement on file so the police could launch the investigation that should have started months ago. "We need to get the ball rolling to find the person responsible for your disappearance. Then, I want to meet my son, hire a security team, and ensure you are both protected 24/7."

Shoving to his feet, he went to the door to the garage and held it open for Caroline. She hurried to follow him, hugging her sweater around her while he helped her into the vehicle. She kept up a steady stream of words as they drove to the Los Altos Hills police station, telling him about the house her father had taken her to in Vancouver for the last five months, and the doctor she'd worked with for her amnesia.

But it was a one-sided conversation. Damon listened with half an ear, still not sure if he could trust what she was telling him, all the while wondering if he should assemble a private team of mercenaries to hunt down whoever had taken her and his unborn child.

For now, he settled for escorting her into the local police station so she could give her statement formally and they could begin legally searching for whoever had abducted her.

They spoke to a detective together and then filled out more paperwork separately. The police assured him they would interrogate her father for providing false information about his contact with Caroline. Damon sincerely hoped that was a felony crime worthy of prison time, but didn't mention as much to his wife. He needed to get a grip on his emotions and figure out his next move.

First, he'd see his son. Bring everyone back to the Los Altos Hills house. Hire security. After that? He would take his family to New York and solicit aid from multibillionaire Malcolm McNeill before the Transparent board meeting. As for Caroline, he couldn't afford to alienate her no matter how much her deception had cost him. More than ever, he needed to get her wedding ring back on her finger so they could raise their child together. If that meant using the attraction between them to his advantage, he would not hesitate. Lucas's future was too important.

He sat with her through her interview with two different officers, one from the Los Altos Hills Police Department and another from the Santa Clara County Sheriff's Department. She kept her composure well, even when she described her kidnappers leaving her alone for weeks while she'd been ill and suffering from dehydration and morning sickness.

The police said they would assign more drive-bys to keep an eye on the property, but Damon had his doubts about the sheriff's department keeping his wife and child safe.

Now, while they waited for an official copy of her statement before leaving the station, Damon reached for her hand and squeezed it. He refused to let her betrayal destroy their marriage.

"I'm eager to meet Lucas after this," Damon said quietly as a uniformed officer wheeled a bicycle past them, a skinny teen trailing behind and muttering curses. "I'll do everything in my power to make sure you both feel safe with me."

The suburban police station had been quiet for most of the morning, but as it neared noon, activity picked up. A young couple came in hand-in-hand to report a stolen car. A confused older woman was released into the custody of a middle-aged man who offered his arm to her for support while they walked out to his car. As Damon watched the two of them leave together, one supporting the other, it occurred to him how at one point he'd found that kind of loving relationship. But it had been a lie.

Unaware of his thoughts, Caroline leaned forward in the molded plastic chair beside him. "The house has better security now than it did a year ago, judging by that massive electronic gate out front, so I'm sure we'll be safe with you. We can pick up Victoria and Lucas as soon as I turn this in." She flipped over the manila folder she was holding. "I miss my baby so much, I don't want to wait another minute."

"*Our* baby," Damon corrected in a tight voice. "Of course you want to see him. And I want to meet him."

Just the thought of that moment hit him in the chest, making each breath hurt as though glass shards were being raked through his insides. "But since your father will look for you here first, I would like to move you and Lucas somewhere safer." He stopped himself as the detective reappeared to take their paperwork. Damon rose to his feet, never relinquishing Caroline's hand.

He would at least play the role of loving husband. He needed her to acknowledge him as Lucas's father and work with him to create a stable environment to raise their child.

After receiving assurances that the department would do "everything possible" to find Caroline's kidnappers, Damon drew her out of the police station and into the noonday sun. Her long shawl swirled around her knees, her high-heeled leather boots clacking on the asphalt as they walked toward the Land Rover.

"Where did you have in mind?" she asked as he helped her into the SUV.

"For starters, I'd like us to take a trip to New York City." He had to restrain himself from buckling her in with his own two hands. What he'd really prefer was an armored car and a few Secret Service guards, but he settled for watching her fasten the seat belt before he closed the door.

"My father knows I kept an apartment in Manhattan," Caroline said as he joined her in the vehicle, where she already had the directions for the rental house she'd taken for her sister and their son pulled up on her phone.

"Dad might look there after he strikes out at the house in Los Altos Hills."

"You wouldn't be staying at your apartment." Damon turned the key in the ignition and pulled out of the parking lot, more than ready to put the cops behind them for the day. "I have family there that I never knew about. Family that's been reaching out to my brothers and me to join the fold. We could stay with them."

Caroline remained silent for a long moment. Damon turned onto a road that led them toward the bay.

"We can stay somewhere else, of course." Damon tried to gauge her expression, realizing she might have lost her ability to trust him to the same debilitating degree that he had lost all trust in her.

They needed to find a way to move past that. Fast.

"My father knows about your connection to the New York McNeills. He showed me an article about your half brother proposing to a ballet dancer he'd never met before, and the public speculation that Malcolm McNeill's will requires his heirs to be married in order to inherit." Caroline folded and refolded her copy of the police statement in fidgety hands.

Her fidgety bare hands.

He needed to put that wedding ring back on her finger where it belonged.

"Does that bother you?" He wasn't sure what to make of her nervousness. "Are you familiar with that family?"

Last year, Damon's father, Liam McNeill, had revealed the existence of his secret sons to his legal heirs and to his father, the wealthy patriarch of the McNeill family and founder of McNeill Resorts, a global hotel chain.

Now, Malcolm had made it his mission in life to bring Damon, Jager and Gabe into the family and make them full heirs. Damon hadn't wanted any part of the reunion until today, when he discovered Stephan Degraff had tried to cheat him out of his son. He was open to leveraging the McNeill muscle for the sake of revenge.

"I've never met any of the McNeills, but my father suggested that Malcolm's will was the only reason you married me, since there are strong tabloid rumors suggesting that he's demanded his heirs be married before inheriting. My father believes you married me to claim your inheritance."

Anger simmered that Stephan Degraff would stoop to that level to undermine their marriage, but by now, it certainly wasn't a surprise. Damon needed the police to dispense justice to his bastard of a father-in-law, sooner rather than later.

"That's not true. I didn't even know I was related to Malcolm when we wed." His grip tightened on the steering wheel. How many more times would he have to have his word verified by the police? "My half brother flew out to Los Altos Hills to introduce himself while I was searching for you in Europe. I didn't learn about the family connection until a private investigator hired by my grandfather located me and convinced me to return to the States a month ago."

On the other side of the Land Rover cab, Caroline gave a small sigh. Of relief or disbelief? He couldn't read her as easily as he once could. She put up major boundaries now.

"Damon, I'm truly sorry. I know this is hard for you. Please remember I have holes in my memory that made it so much easier for my father to persuade me. It's still difficult to sift through my life and trust my gut." She put the police report aside and double-checked the GPS on her phone before settling the device in front of the map screen built into the dashboard so he could see where they were going. "But I promise you, I am trying to make sense of what happened. Maybe it wouldn't be a bad idea to go to New York. A change of scenery might be good for both of us."

The audio on the GPS alerted him his final turn was ahead.

Time to meet his son.

And as much as he couldn't wait to hold his child in his arms, Damon couldn't help but wish that the circumstances were very, very different.

Anxious to see her baby again, Caroline texted Victoria as they pulled up to the carriage house she'd rented for her sister and son. Before she could open the door of the Land Rover and race inside to hold Lucas again, Damon placed a hand on her knee.

It was a touch designed purely to slow her down. She could tell by his body language that he had withdrawn from her. Ever since she'd told him about the baby, Damon had been cooler toward her. Yes, he'd accompanied her to the police station and said all the right things about protecting her and Lucas. But she could feel his retreat as surely as a cold front coming off the Pacific.

"Let's take a look at the cars parked nearby first," he suggested, adjusting the rearview mirror for a better view of the street. "Make sure we don't see one of your father's vehicles, or anyone who looks like they're sitting idle and keeping an eye on the place."

Her stomach cramped; it worried her that she hadn't thought to do so on her own. What if her memory loss was affecting her judgement more than she realized? The possibility made her think she might need to rely on Damon more, for Lucas's safety. "Good idea."

"I'm going to hire full-time security for you and Lucas as soon as we get home, but until I've got a team in place, we need to be careful."

"Right." She nodded, a fierce wave of protectiveness surging at the thought of someone trying to take Lucas away. "Thank you for thinking of that."

"If I had any idea you might be at risk, I would have done it a year ago." He let himself out of the SUV and came around to open her door.

She took the hand he held out to her and met his gaze as he helped her down to the sidewalk. A pleasurable frisson danced over her skin from the contact. Because he'd offered to protect her? Or maybe because for the first time since she'd returned to Los Altos Hills, she wasn't keeping secrets from him?

Whatever it was, the sensation reminded her of a time before their relationship had become a casualty of her kidnapping. But telling Damon the truth about how she was hiding his son from him had driven a wedge between them, thwarting any attempt to salvage their marriage.

When Damon let go of her hand, he placed a palm on her back, guiding her up the stone path to the two-story brick carriage house. His touch was impersonal, perfunctory. It was the same courtesy he'd extend to anyone in a weakened condition. So she needed to stop feeling pleasure at the contact, and at the way his leg sometimes brushed hers.

Ahead of them, the blinds were all drawn on the oversize lower windows, as Caroline had requested. But her sister must have had a way to see outside because the heavy wooden front door swung wide open before they even had a chance to knock.

"Caroline!" Victoria wore black-and-pink plaid pajama pants and a gray Stanford tee, her dark brown hair in a ponytail drooping sideways, the tail tickling along Lucas's forehead while the baby slept in her arms. "Thank God you're here. I saw someone's shadow near the kitchen window about an hour ago and I panicked, thinking Dad found us."

Victoria gave her sister a one-armed hug, skillfully keeping her precious cargo safe on the opposite side of her body while she squeezed Caroline tight. Damon's gaze went to the baby, but he didn't reach for Lucas yet.

"I'll go look around back. You should go inside and lock the door behind you." Damon shifted away, taking another wary glance around the quiet yard. There were no houses close by, just the huge, three-story stone home that went with the carriage house. The property bordered a park with a playground on one side where a couple of young mothers pushed preschool-aged children on the swings.

"Oh, wow." Victoria edged out of the doorway a bit to watch Damon as he strode away. "He's even hotter in person."

Too bad Caroline's very hot husband had retreated from her in every way possible.

"Agreed," she said, gently lifting her son from Victoria's arms, savoring the warm weight of his tiny body wrapped in a blanket covered with elephants. "We can ogle him from a window though, once we're inside."

For a moment, Lucas's face scrunched like he was about to cry, but then he settled in against Caroline's chest, his tiny hand stretching and flexing before relaxing against his face. She kissed his temple, rubbing her cheek along the silky down of dark hair that covered his head. He smelled like baby shampoo.

While she cuddled him, Victoria watched Damon from one window and then another, discreetly peering through the blinds. The house had been beautifully restored, with the original pine floors buffed to glowing.

A wrought iron chandelier hung from the exposed joist ceiling in the living room, where a fire burned in the stone hearth. Blue baby blankets and equipment were strewn around, making the place looked lived-in, but not messy. Then again, maybe seeing all of her child's things simply made her happy, so she welcomed the sight of baby chaos.

When Damon came back around to the front entrance, Victoria was waiting to open the door again for him. Caroline watched him as he stepped inside and drew the bolt behind him.

"I'm Victoria, by the way." Her sister stuck out a hand to introduce herself, planting herself in front of Damon. "Caroline's sister. And I'm going to start packing so you can meet the kiddo."

"Nice to meet you." He gave a clipped, polite nod, even though his eyes were completely locked on Lucas. Damon could be charming when he chose to be, but he'd always been reserved around women, as if his smart brain was too busy thinking about his next revolutionary tech idea instead of flirting.

Caroline wondered if any woman had turned his head in the past months that he'd thought she'd left him. The idea sparked a jealous heat that she didn't want to acknowledge right now. Not when she needed to introduce him to his son.

Listening to her sister's footsteps as she retreated up the stairs, Caroline brought Lucas over to meet his father.

"Damon, this is Lucas." She turned her body so that her back was to her husband, giving him the best view of their sleeping child from over her shoulder.

She could feel Damon go very still behind her. Peering around to look up at him, she spotted the awe in his expression. The wonder. The feeling resonated with her. Weeks after giving birth to Lucas she still experienced that same sense of amazement every time she looked at their baby.

"He's perfect." Damon brushed a hand over Lucas's downy head. "Thank you for bringing him to me. For taking a chance on trusting me again." He made no mention of trusting her in return. "I will keep you both safe."

"I know you will." She just wished she felt more sure of his reasons for marrying her. He had said he didn't even know about his grandfather, let alone the dictate that the McNeill heirs marry to inherit, when he'd proposed to her. But after all that had happened in the last months, she would need to work to recover her faith in their bond. "Do you remember why I named him Lucas?"

Damon traced the sleeping infant's features, running his thumb along one barely-there eyebrow, his fingers along one baby-fat cheek. "We came up with names the day we decided to throw away your birth control pills, right after the wedding."

"I know we were just sort of goofing around that night, but—" With the baby cradled against her, her shrug was awkward. "It was the only thing I had to go on for choosing a name."

"I wasn't joking that night." He slid around to face her, putting his arm around her shoulder to draw her closer. "Chloe for a girl. Lucas for a boy."

"Good. It was hard naming him on my own, when I was still so unsure of so much." She felt some tension slip out of her shoulders that she hadn't realized she'd been feeling.

"I would never question a decision you made for our child when you were ill, alone and had no support." He cupped her face in his hand, his tone grave, his gaze cool and remote despite the supportive words. "I'm damned sorry I wasn't there for you. For both of you."

She nodded stiffly, not wanting tears to spoil a moment that should be happy.

"Thank you." She attempted a smile to lighten the mood, but couldn't quite manage it. Instead, she lifted Lucas higher and edged her arms closer to Damon. "Would you like to hold him while I help Victoria pack up his things?"

"Yes." He reached for the baby, sliding one arm under Lucas while using the other to carefully cradle him. "It's past time I got to know our son."

Caroline lingered, unable to tear her eyes away from the sight of their baby finally nestled in his father's arms. Heart in her throat, she could hardly speak. She bit her lip hard to collect herself.

"You look like a natural." She tucked the blanket

around Lucas's toes, her knuckles grazing Damon's bicep.

"Gabe had a son last spring, while you were…away." Damon's jaw tensed. "His girlfriend gave him full custody before breaking things off a few months afterward. I got to hold Jason a few times." Turning his attention back to Lucas, Damon pushed the blanket away from the baby's face. "The boys have a strong resemblance."

"All the McNeill males do." She had seen the photos of his half brothers Quinn, Ian and Cameron in the article her father had shown her. Their blue eyes, dark hair, and tall, athletic builds were strikingly similar to Jager, Damon and Gabe's.

"Lucas won't lack for cousins. Cameron just adopted his wife's daughter, Isla." He glanced back up at Caroline. "You'll meet them when we go to New York."

"How soon?" She was nervous about her father finding them. To work off some of the anxiety, she started picking up the baby items strewn around the living area. A soft rattle with a puppy face. An empty bottle. "And do you think it's safe for Victoria to return to school?"

"We can leave for New York as soon as you're ready. I'll hire security for Victoria for the next six weeks to make sure she's safe. I can have someone in place to accompany her by late this afternoon if she wants to drive back tomorrow."

Caroline nodded, grateful for the way he easily accepted responsibility for her sister.

Victoria hurried down the stairs with a pink duffel bag over one shoulder, her tennis shoes half on and untied. "Whoa. Whoa. Whoa. Let's not get too carried away making plans for other peoples' lives, okay? I don't need a keeper, thank you very much." She paused at the bottom of the stairs to shove her feet more fully into her shoes, jamming the laces down inside with her socks.

Caroline carried the empty bottle over to the sink and washed it. "I couldn't live with myself if something happened to you because of me. You can handle a bodyguard for a few weeks until we figure out who kidnapped me and why." She'd never forget the way her captors had threatened her siblings. Those threats had frightened her far more than anything they'd done to her. "I'm scared enough about our younger brothers, but the police promised to get in touch with their boarding schools to make sure they were on alert."

"Seriously?" Victoria let her bag fall to the floor with a thunk. "I've got way too much research to do this semester. I'll be lucky to ever leave the library. And I'm going to be stuck with some muscle-head goon?"

She was twenty-four years old to Caroline's twenty-eight, but sometimes Caroline felt decades older.

"You might come to appreciate muscle if it saves you from being dragged away from your home and held against your will." Caroline shoved the clean bottle into the diaper bag along with a few baby towels. "Trust me."

Victoria hesitated. "I know, but—"

Barreling past her sister, Caroline headed toward

the door, unwilling to hear complaints about the extra protection they all needed. "Once we have the car seat and the porta-crib, we'll be all set to go."

"I can get them." Damon passed her the baby, his hand grazing her breast and setting off a riot of sensations. "Wait here and I'll pack the vehicle."

Their gazes met, heat sparking in a whole other, unspoken conversation going on between them. What a crazy moment to recall that her obstetrician had okayed her to resume all normal activity at her last visit. The printed patient summary she'd taken home had specifically referred to physical intimacy. Clearly, her body had gotten the message.

"I—" She couldn't even remember what they'd been talking about. "Er. Okay?"

If there were any doubts in her mind that they were both feeling the spark, they faded away at the heated look in Damon's eyes. Was it the deliberate, calculated seduction of a man who wanted to keep his family together? Or was he feeling a genuine attraction? The hitch in her breathing made her heartbeat skip.

"Good." He pressed a kiss to her cheek, using it as a way to speak quietly into her ear. "I'm very ready to take you home."

# Six

After cueing up the playlist Caroline had requested on the house's built-in state-of-the-art sound system, Damon adjusted the settings so that the nursery was the only room to hear the classical lullaby music. Tapping the app on his phone, he turned down the volume, settling on a barely-there level so Lucas could fall asleep to the soft symphonies.

Meeting his son had helped him to quiet some of the anger still simmering inside him over his wife's deception. Seeing the boy's face had raised the stakes. He couldn't afford to fail at this marriage. So while he had no intention of giving over his heart to Caroline again, he would fulfill his obligations to her. He would be attentive. Solicitous. And he would damn well be passionate. His attraction to her hadn't dimmed.

They'd all been busy since returning home from the rental house with the baby and Caroline's sister. Damon had spent time researching private security firms, calling friends for recommendations before settling on a company based in San Jose. It had been started by a former local sheriff with the help of the tech guru who owned a digital security firm called Fortress. Damon used the system on his own properties and had been impressed with Fortress's founder, Zach Chance, who had given him some welcome input on start-ups in Silicon Valley when Damon first arrived in town. Damon liked having a personal connection to the business at a time when he was questioning who he could really trust in his life.

Once he'd signed a contract and emailed it back, it was less than an hour before the first shift team arrived. They upgraded some of the exterior security systems on the Los Altos Hills property, then divided the protective detail so two people would remain with Caroline and Lucas at all times, and one guard would go to Stanford with Victoria.

They were all scheduled to leave in the morning, with Damon, Caroline and the baby on a private flight to New York, while Victoria made the short drive to her university. Now that the arrangements were set, Damon could relax enough to help put his son to bed for the first time.

His son.

Rejoining Caroline over the porta-crib in a room they'd designated as the nursery, Damon watched as she expertly laid the swaddled bundle on the freshly washed sheets she'd pulled out of the dryer a few minutes ago. Dinosaurs cartwheeled around the border of the blanket. Lucas's baby hand clutched the satin trim of the cover, his grip sporadic and unintentional. He seemed to be at an age where he flexed his fingers simply to make use of them. His stare was vacant and sleepy for a moment before he closed his eyes again.

"He's a miracle," Damon said earnestly. He continued to watch the baby drift into a deeper sleep, his tiny hand falling lightly on the mattress beside his nose. "I need to make up for a lot of lost time with him."

"You could always…take the late shift for his next feeding," Caroline offered haltingly, as if she wasn't sure how much labor to share. Or how much he wanted to take part in parenting.

No doubt about it, they were tentative around each other now, though she did seem more relaxed since they'd retrieved the baby. It was obvious that motherhood made her happy. She might not have feelings for him anymore, but Damon had no doubt that she loved their child profoundly. She practically glowed when she looked at Lucas.

Damon wasn't sure if that was a normal connection, or if her attachment was all the stronger because of what she'd gone through during her pregnancy. He'd read her official statement, the detached summary of facts not doing justice to the hell she must have gone through. The fear. Loneliness. Confusion. Of course, there was no "statement" for him to read about her experience afterward with her father. How much had Stephan De-graff added to his daughter's fears by keeping her in the dark about her marriage? How could anyone let their daughter think she was alone in parenting a newborn when she had a husband desperately searching for her?

"I'll gladly take the late shift." He relished the quiet time in the dim nursery with her now after a day that had come at him from all sides. "It will give me a chance to get to know him."

"I'm going to take you up on that." She moved toward the night-light and switched it to a lower setting. "Having Victoria babysit him the last two days has helped me catch up on rest, I think. I feel better than when I left my father's house."

"All the more reason to secure some help with him." Damon had brought in two potential nanny candidates and asked Caroline to interview them while he dealt with the security team. Caroline had liked them both, but insisted she wanted to care for Lucas on her own. "An extra caregiver could give you much needed time to recover from the pregnancy and the ordeal you've been through."

He followed her to the door and closed it partially behind them while Caroline paused in the hallway to pull up the nursery monitor's video feed on her phone.

"I realize that." She tucked the phone in the pocket of her shawl sweater, flipping her ponytail behind her shoulder. "But I like caring for him myself. Being with him."

"And I admire that. But you'll have more energy to enjoy him if you're taking good care of yourself. But we can debate this another time." He opted for a strategic temporary retreat on the subject rather than risk backing her into a corner. Damon pointed toward the second-story patio that she liked, hoping he could persuade her to unwind with him for a while. He needed to make his case to recommit to their marriage. "I had some of that herbal tea you like brought out near the fire pit if you want to stargaze before bed."

"You did?" She tipped her head to one side to look out toward the patio where flames leaped from the copper bowl. "That sounds good, actually. Thank you."

Her careful politeness bothered him. It reminded him of his own hesitation. No doubt about it, there was an awkwardness between them now. A cool wariness behind the facade.

"We have a lot to talk about before tomorrow." He pushed open the French doors from the master suite's sitting room that led to the patio. "But I don't want to wear you out."

"I'll be fine." She stopped to look up at the sky, tipping her head back to see the stars while a cool breeze blew the hem of her sweater against him. "So much happened today, my head is still spinning."

There had been a time when he would have wrapped his arms around her to steady her. To kiss her until they were both breathless and ready for more.

"Mine, too." He limited himself to putting a hand on her waist, gently guiding her toward the daybed swing where he'd piled blankets in deference to the cold night air. "I found out I had a son today."

Her guilty wince made it clear she was still feeling wary around him.

The patio heaters were humming, along with the fire. Decorative stonework along the low walls of the exterior was punctuated with built-in propane torches. The effect was medieval, making the home look all the more like an old French château.

"I'm sorry that my father's lies cost us the chance to be together for Lucas's birth." She stopped in front of the daybed and held the chain to steady it while she sat down.

The glow of firelight played along her skin, brightening her cheeks.

"Yes. They did." Damon took his time unfurling the blankets and tucking them around her, not wanting to get sucked into a conversation about Stephan Degraff. Damon needed this time to mend his relationship with her. Regardless of what her motives had been in hiding Lucas from him, or deceiving him about her condition, Damon needed to win her over. Earn back her trust so they could move forward in parenting their son. Together.

He would not raise his own child in the type of unstable environment he'd known growing up.

"I don't how Dad could have done that to me. Was he trying to teach me a lesson for marrying someone he didn't approve of?" She slipped off her boots and tucked her feet under her on the swing, sitting cross-legged. She laid her phone on the cushion beside her, leaving the video feed from the nursery monitor on. "Or did he hope I'd just forget about the marriage forever if he pretended it didn't exist? Did he really expect you would never find out I was still alive? God, what if one of us had wanted to get married again. Would he have just stood aside and allow a bigamous union?"

"Tough to know what he was thinking." Damon took the spot beside her then leaned forward to retrieve the insulated tea carafe. He poured two mugs of the stuff even though he wasn't much of a tea drinker. Anything to get her to stay here with him for a little while.

And since bashing her father wasn't going to get him anywhere with her, he would remain diplomatic. For now. Sooner or later, she would have to discover his plans to ruin Stephan Degraff. By then, Damon intended to have their marriage on far more stable ground.

She wrapped her hands around the gray stoneware mug and sipped the steaming hot drink. He took the opportunity to change the subject. Setting down his cup, he reached into the pocket of the sports jacket he'd worn for his meetings with the new security team members and took out her wedding ring set. He held the rings up to the firelight so she could see.

"One of the pieces of evidence the police pointed to in support of your father's claim that you walked out on me was the fact that you left this behind." He'd had the princess-cut diamond engagement ring and the matching platinum-and-diamond wedding band custom-made for her.

He studied her expression carefully, trying to assess what he saw there. Nostalgia? Maybe. But there was wariness, too. Had she taken it off when she got home that day, planning to leave him?

"I wondered where they went." Caroline set down her tea on the stone rim of the copper fire bowl, then reached to touch the glittering band, tracing the outline with one finger. "I thought they were stolen from me while I was drugged."

Taking her other hand, he dropped the rings into her palm and the diamonds sent tiny refractions glinting in the dark.

She stared down at the rings, making no move to put them on her finger.

"Do you think you were wearing them that day?"

She peered up at him, surprised. "I would have worn them on the plane coming home from Heathrow. I'm sure I had them on when I was taken from the house."

"The rings were on the top of the bureau in my closet. As if you left them there deliberately for me to find."

"I suppose I could be wrong." She shook her head

slowly. "I was given a lot of drugs during those first two weeks. More when they moved me a month after that. But I'm not sure I'll ever recall exactly how that day played out when they took me."

He ground his teeth in frustration, knowing he needed to get past it fast if he wanted to fix things with Caroline. He wanted the ring on her finger, needed her commitment to this marriage to provide a healthy and happy childhood for Lucas.

"You may never recover all your memories," he reminded himself as much as her. "But I hope you'll consider working with a new therapist in New York. Recalling those lost memories isn't just about the two of us. It's important for Lucas."

Caroline rubbed the two rings against one another, sliding the platinum-and-diamond pieces back and forth between two fingers.

"You can't imagine how badly I want answers." Her brown eyes reflected the glow of the fire as she glanced up at him. "I need to know what happened, so yes, of course I'll meet a new doctor."

In this much, at least, they were on the same page.

More than that, he recognized the vibrant energy and determination in that statement. It was a flicker from the past; for a moment, he spied the woman he'd fallen in love with inside this stranger who'd returned to him.

"Good." He closed his hand around hers where she toyed with the rings, stilling the movement long enough to take the jewelry from her. "Then, with your permission, I'd like to return these to where they belong."

Wordlessly, she watched him line up the bands and hold them over her left hand. The swing swayed gently beneath them, lulling them to forget some of the angst of their hellish day. Still, a furrow wrinkled her brow just above her nose, as if she couldn't quite decide.

He tipped her chin up with his free hand, needing to see that fire in her eyes again.

"All I'm asking for is the chance to start over." He spoke gently, knowing this had been tough on her, too. He didn't know how much he could trust her, but he damned well needed to try to move past her betrayal. "To try and be a couple again." He nudged the phone beside her, the video feed from the nursery brightening for a moment to show their sleeping child. "For Lucas's sake."

He knew it was the final words that persuaded her. She gave the slightest nod before returning her gaze to her bare finger as he slid the wedding band set back into place.

Memories of the vows they'd spoken hit him hard. He could hear her voice from the past promising to love him forever and always. For the rest of her days.

He'd believed her absolutely.

Disillusionment left a chill the roaring fire couldn't touch. Having accomplished his goal for the night, he celebrated the victory by placing a cool kiss on the back of her hand just above the rings. He was ready to finish his drink and retire for the night, to figure out his next move once they got to New York.

And yes, to take his time staring at his child and wrapping his brain around this massive change in his life.

Straightening, he was surprised to see the soft glow of heat in Caroline's eyes, the relaxed parting of her lips. He watched in stunned fascination as she canted forward. Toward him.

All around them, the night sounds intensified. A few brave birds called out and the logs crackled and shifted, casting sparks on the stone patio deck nearby. Caroline's breath puffed against his lips for one sexy exhale before her hands clamped his shoulders.

He had a moment to breathe in the strawberry scent of her lip balm. Then her mouth landed on his with a delicate and wholly unexpected kiss.

Caroline didn't know what came over her.

Simple attraction to her husband? Or was it a memory of true love inspired by the wedding rings he'd carefully slid into place on her left hand?

She didn't know. But the compulsion to get closer, to test the swirl of complicated feelings sending pleasure to every atom of her being, was too strong to ignore.

How long had it been since she'd experienced something so...delicious?

Her tentative exploration of Damon's lips didn't last long. A breath. An instant. Then his hands came around her waist, drawing her whole body toward him, as if he could encompass all of her with one squeeze of his powerful arms.

The pleasure she'd been feeling multiplied ten times. A hundred times. Being pressed up against her husband's muscular warmth sent tingly sensations everywhere from her breasts to her thighs, with the most potent concentration deep inside her. Being in his arms, kissing him, felt more like coming home than crossing the threshold of this colorless mansion ever had.

This, she recognized.

This, she remembered in her body more than her brain.

How else could she account for the sudden, reflexive *need*? Her hands tunneled into his dark hair, and she craved more. More of the kiss and the man.

He accommodated her instantly, pulling her fully across his lap. Her thighs draped over his, her hip pressed intimately to his arousal. The chilly night air blew lightly on her back, but it didn't cool the heat their bodies generated where they touched. Damon kissed her with a slow thoroughness that undid her. She dropped her hands to his chest, wanting to feel the thrum of his heartbeat, to see if the rhythm was as unsteady as hers. Or maybe just to reassure herself this was no fevered dream or wishful memory.

Damon McNeill in her arms was the real thing.

She broke the kiss, needing to feel that addictive slide of his mouth on her neck. Behind her ear. Down to the

base of her throat. She didn't know if she steered him
there or he simply understood everything she wanted.
Arching into him, she let the heat build, not questioning it. Needing it.

He said he wanted to start over, didn't he?

Was it madness to begin again this way, right here
and now?

For the first time in months, she didn't have to strug-
gle to remember. She could simply be. Feel.

Savor.

She tugged at the buttons on her sweater, needing to
feel his kiss on her breasts. He thumbed aside the bra
strap as she exposed it, his hands working seamlessly
beside hers...

Until the wail of Lucas's cry filled the night.

The nursery monitor feed blinked to brighter life
on her phone, the audio as clear as if they were standing right next to the crib. Caroline lurched forward, off
Damon's lap.

He stood beside her.

"Get your rest, Caroline." He placed a kiss on her
forehead. "I want to go to Lucas."

She couldn't argue since she'd already teased him
about taking the late feeding. Damon deserved to spend
time with Lucas after she'd kept him to herself these
last weeks. Logically, she understood that.

But as she watched Damon walk away from her, she
got the sense that he hadn't just left to be with his son.
He'd left to get away from her and what was happening

between them. Because no matter what he said about new beginnings, she knew he didn't trust her.

And it was possible he didn't even love her.

So no matter how blissfully sensual his kisses made her feel, she would be wise to keep her guard up around her husband.

# Seven

By late afternoon the next day, Damon sat beside Caroline in the back of a limousine taking them from the airport to his grandfather's home on the Upper East Side of Manhattan. Lucas snoozed in a car seat across from them while their security guard rode up front with the driver. Malcolm McNeill insisted on sending the Mercedes limo for them, even though he was out of the country on business. When Damon had called his grandfather to let him know they were going to be in New York City, the old man had urged them to stay at his house since it was fully staffed and none of the McNeills were in town for the next three days.

Damon had accepted since he needed to meet with his grandfather as soon as possible to discuss the

McNeills taking over Stephan Degraff's stake in Transparent. He'd closed the house in Los Altos Hills that morning, but asked his Realtor not to put the property on the market yet. His life had changed drastically since Caroline's return. He now had his wife and his son to consider, making the Silicon Valley condo he'd rented out of the question because it was too small. Plus, there was her long-term safety to consider. As much as he wished they could hole up back on the family property in Martinique, he knew she wouldn't go for that.

But sooner or later, he wanted his son to meet Jager and Gabe.

Now that his brothers were recognizing their father's relatives as family—though not their father himself, if Damon had anything to say about it—Damon needed to get used to the idea that he had half brothers. And he'd soon have to introduce Caroline to them. Their son deserved a stronger sense of family than he and Caroline could provide. And he had no intention of allowing Stephan Degraff anywhere near his child.

"I'm anxious to see your grandfather's home." She shifted in her seat, straightening her long wool coat to cover her legs as she peered out the window. The car sped up on a curving road through Central Park. "If it's as big as you say, it's got to be one of those turn-of-the-century mansions on the Upper East Side."

He pulled his gaze up from her legs, from the spot where her tall leather boots met the hem of her knee-length skirt. He'd thought about their kiss all night, wondering if it had surprised her as much as him. Not that he was caught off guard by the heat or the passion. He expected as much when they touched. It had always been that way between them. What had stunned him was how engaged she'd been in the kiss. The touches. He'd missed that about her. The woman who'd returned to their doorstep, claiming not to know him, was more circumspect. But something had reawakened her more impulsive side and he wondered how long it would take for him to see that side of her again.

"The McNeill home is impressive." With an effort, he focused on her words instead of the attraction. Damon wasn't as much of an architecture aficionado as Gabe, who was bringing his historic hotel back to pristine life in Martinique. But he'd been around enough five-star properties across the world to appreciate something like the McNeill mansion. "It has six floors, not counting the staff rooms and kitchen on the basement level. There's an entrance to the park across the street."

"How long did you spend there?" She smoothed her hands along the folded leather gloves on her lap, her wedding rings glinting in the dull winter sunlight.

He'd been glad to see the bands back in place today when she'd awoken from a long rest. Damon had kept his word where Lucas was concerned the night before, walking the baby around the house when he cried and settling him down after the midnight bottle. He'd enjoyed the time to study the boy's features and get to know him even though the feeding had interrupted one hell of a moment with Caroline. There would be more heated moments. Soon.

"I only stayed there for a few days last month after my grandfather's private investigator found me over in Europe." He'd been in a dark place at the time, convinced Caroline had either left him or was being held against her will. "My brother, Jager, had been looking for me. I'd saddled him with the responsibility of overseeing Transparent while I was away and he was beginning to have trouble explaining my absence to investors. I threw out my cell phone though, not wanting to deal with any of it." A foolish act. "If only I'd kept it, maybe we would have been together sooner."

The car slowed for another light. A few heavy snowflakes began to fall, lightly brushing the windows on their way to the ground. The city was expecting major winter weather tonight, and he would be glad to get his family settled for the night.

It still floored him to think about having a family of his own.

"At least we're together now, and Lucas is safe." Her dark gaze landed on the baby as the little boy stretched and sighed. "Thank you for making sure Victoria got to school safely, too." She checked her phone and then set it aside. "I told her to text me if she heard from Dad, but she said everything seemed fine at her apartment."

Damon nodded. "I'm receiving updates from her protective detail, as well. They retrieved a few books and personal items from the building on campus, and moved her temporarily to a spot with more security. Just until the police finish investigating your father's role in this."

They could only do so much to hide Victoria if her father wanted to see her, but at least she wouldn't be easy to find.

"I'm more concerned about protecting her from whoever kidnapped me. My captors threatened to come after my siblings if I didn't cooperate." She turned her attention back toward the sleeping infant. "I want them safe, and Lucas, too." She tugged at the green striped quilt she'd laid over the car seat to keep him warm, lifting it higher.

Damon wanted to tell her to prepare herself for the possibility that her father was more involved in her kidnapping than she realized. But perhaps Caroline herself had asked for her father's help in freeing her from marriage to Damon and simply didn't remember. Better to keep his misgivings to himself and let the police work on it.

And his private investigators. He'd called Bentley—the PI who'd located Damon when he'd been wandering Europe looking for Caroline—with an update the night before when he'd been pacing the floor with Lucas. Like Damon, Bentley was suspicious of Stephan's role in Caroline's disappearance.

Until he had proof, however, Damon's revenge against Stephan would wait. He'd spend his time assembling all the pieces necessary to ruin him so he would be ready to act when the time came.

For now, Damon would focus on solidifying his relationship with his wife. After last night's heated kiss, the plan was very, very appealing.

Two hours later, Caroline wandered through the sixth-floor solarium of the stunning house that belonged to Damon's grandfather. Snow fell in a dizzying haze on the glass roof, which was illuminated by the ambient light from Central Park on the opposite side of Fifth Avenue. The building faced East 76th Street, but she could see the park from here.

Lucas had already been settled in his own bedroom across from hers on the fifth floor. She was touched to see the steps the household staff had taken on short notice to ready the room for a baby. They kept a crib in storage, apparently, and had set it up for them. It had been in use often as of late, since Cameron McNeill, one of Damon's half brothers, had recently adopted his wife's daughter.

Caroline had gotten the full scoop from two fresh-faced staffers who were pursuing advanced degrees in early childhood education—young women recently retained to work part-time whenever Malcolm McNeill hosted the grandchildren he hoped would soon fill his home. Like the Mercedes limo he'd sent to the airport and the home he'd opened to Caroline and Damon unconditionally, the extra caregivers were another way Malcolm proved extremely generous and thoughtful.

Caroline hadn't wanted to deprive the young women

of the new charge they seemed excited to care for. When she'd left him in the nursery, he was on a blanket in the middle of the thickly carpeted floor, surrounded by blocks and rattles, his every coo and cry tended to by Marcie and Dana. Curious, she now took out her phone to see the nursery monitor feed, and the group was just as she'd left them. Classical music played while Lucas stared up at a baby gym, the young women flying stuffed toys above him to keep him entertained.

Nearby, the elevator doors swished open, alerting her to company. Caroline turned from the view to look out into the hallway through the open door.

Damon approached her, his strong shoulders backlit by the sconces flanking the elevator. He'd changed from the suit he'd worn for their flight. The gray jacket and dark jeans were more casual, the white shirt with no tie a staple look for him. He'd traded his black tie-up dress shoes for boots.

He looked good enough to eat. No doubt that's why she felt the need to study every inch of him. She was willing to bet he smelled great, too. She had dreamed of that sandalwood and spice scent when she'd been apart from him.

"Is everything all right?" he asked, edging around a café table in the center of the solarium. "I've been looking all over for you."

"I'm fine." She lowered herself to sit on a bright-blue modern sofa in front of the window looking down onto the street. "This is like being at the drive-in theater.

Only the show playing is *New York in a Snowstorm*."
She gestured to the wide view framed by long glass
panels.

Just hearing Damon's footsteps on the tile floor made
her skin hum with awareness. How was she supposed to
be on her guard around him with no baby in her arms
to care for? No distractions of any kind?

Her main goals in New York were keeping her child
safe and finding out if Damon had married her out of
self-interest. The former seemed easier now with a
full-time bodyguard devoted to Lucas. And the latter?
She wouldn't be able to discover much until Malcolm
McNeill returned to the town house. Or maybe Damon's half brothers. In the meantime, her husband had
made it clear he wanted to start over. Be a couple again.

The memory of his words last night slid over her
senses like a caress, making her shiver.

"I can light a fire if you're cold." Damon hesitated
at the edge of the sofa, pointing toward the hearth on
the other side of the room.

"No, thank you." She realized her mistake as soon
as she said it, since he took the opportunity to sit down
beside her, bringing all that masculine appeal within
inches of her. If she'd taken him up on his offer to build
a fire, she would have had more time to build her defenses. "You can see the view better this way. That's
why I didn't bother to turn a light on."

"I wondered why you were sitting in the dark." He
kept his attention on the snow coming down, the fat

flakes gathering up in the corners of the windowpanes, outlining the view with a frosty border.

"Just soaking up a side of New York I've never seen. The year I worked in the Financial District, I lived down there and barely ventured north of Canal Street." She clung to a neutral conversational topic, safe terrain after the emotional toll of every exchange the day before. "My building was in an old part of the city, but construction was completed the year I moved in. It couldn't be more different from this place."

The neo-Renaissance mansion that housed the McNeill patriarch was a turn-of-the-century masterpiece. It even had its own Wikipedia page.

Damon shifted to make himself more comfortable, extending his arm along the back of the sofa just behind her neck. Not touching her. Just…so close. She breathed in the light hint of sandalwood.

"How did you like living here?" he asked, and she felt the warmth of his gaze on her even though she kept her attention on the living snow globe outside the window. "I don't think we've ever talked about that. I know you grew up in San Francisco. Got your degree in Boston. What did you think of New York City?"

"I loved it." She remembered the joy of earning her own paycheck, and a good one at that. "Coming from a wealthy family, I always felt a bit guilty for having nice things that I didn't earn for myself." She had noticed at college the vast difference between kids who were sent to the prestigious school because of their family name and finances, versus the handful of students who were genuinely brilliant and there on scholarship. "But when I lived in New York, I had a sense of independence that I'd never really felt before. I got the job on my own merit and did it well."

She'd always thought she would return, in fact. She'd kept her apartment on Spruce Street and sublet it since then.

"What made you give it up?" Damon asked. He trailed a finger along her shoulder, a light touch with a powerful impact through the simple cashmere sweater dress she'd changed into after the plane trip.

Keen awareness of that touch made it difficult to concentrate. But did he touch her out of desire? Or a more calculated need to reset the relationship button?

"My father asked me come work for him and help him choose which businesses to invest in." At the time, she'd felt obligated to fulfill the request since she couldn't have afforded her college education on her own. "I felt underqualified, and worried he only gave me the job out of family loyalty, but I helped him turn an excellent profit on the two companies he invested in before I got involved in the deal with Transparent."

She hadn't thought much about returning to her career since leaving Mexico. And yes, she wanted to be a full-time mother to enjoy every moment with Lucas that she could. But would it restore some of her personal confidence, her faith in herself, if she worked on a part-time basis?

"If we hadn't started a relationship, would you still have recommended your father invest in Transparent?"

"Without question." She had recovered her memories of the earliest part of their dating first, and she felt certain about her answer. "I knew within the first week that I would endorse it. There was a good energy in the building. Everyone really bought into your ideas." She hadn't recommended it that quickly, of course, spending time on the due diligence to make sure the market forecasts and business plans made sense.

But she'd had a strong instinct about the company early on.

"Were you concerned that I wouldn't be the best CEO to take the company to the next level?"

Straightening, she shook off the allure of his touch and the cozy sensation of watching the snowfall. "Should I look back at my notes? Because I'm getting the impression that there is more to your questions than just casual conversation."

"You still have your notes?" He lifted a dark eyebrow.

She met his gaze, but she detected only curiosity. Professional interest. She felt a new buzz along her skin that had less to do with attraction and more to do with her work. She'd forgotten the excitement of being a part of a new project, and helping to bring a brilliant idea to life.

"Of course. I did extensive research on your software, from the technical production plans to marketing."

She hadn't given much thought to Transparent since her marriage. So much had happened in her personal life—from the kidnapping to becoming a mother—that her job was the least of her concerns. But there'd been a time where she lived and breathed her career. "And you must remember that I shared those reports—over a year ago—with my father, since that was part of the terms of his investment."

"Certainly." Damon nodded thoughtfully and she recognized that look of deep concentration. When he turned back toward her, his gaze hardened. He was all business. "I had my software tested by a hacker recently, and he discovered a few holes I need to plug before we release it."

"I'm confused. What does that have to do with my old notes?"

"Nothing." Damon shifted closer, the blue leather cushion creaking softly as his knee brushed against hers. "But if I know the extent of the research on Transparent your father has access to, I might be able to shift the final product to ensure he can't ambush it once it hits the market."

"He wouldn't—" She stopped herself as she saw Damon's gaze darken. Even in the dim glow of light reflected from the street lamps outside, she could see the glint of frustration in his eyes. "Okay, maybe he would."

"Do you really believe that, Caroline? Or are you just saying it for my sake?" His words were clipped, his tone brusque.

"I understand that he resents you for marrying me." She didn't comprehend the depth of her father's fury with Damon, however. She remembered his adamant refusal to attend their wedding. "I know he was frustrated with you before we even met, because you wouldn't accept his help or expertise—only his financial support."

"I made it clear that's all I needed."

She recalled how Damon's intractable ways angered her dad. "He's used to being a valuable asset when he supports a new business."

Damon abruptly rose from the couch. He stalked the short distance to the windows overlooking the street. "Not to me. I wouldn't let him beat me at business. But then it got much, much worse when he realized I'd won you, too."

The words hit her with unexpected force. She shot to her feet to face him.

"I'm not a prize for the taking, Damon." Fuming, she folded her arms.

"And that's not how I see you. But make no mistake, your father views your affection for me as a betrayal." He shook his head. "I don't understand it, but nothing else can explain the way he tried to shut me out of Lucas's life. The way he misled the police when you disappeared."

Caroline didn't want to believe it. Her head hurt just thinking about all the ways her dad had tried to keep her and Damon apart. Had her therapist been correct when she gently suggested she'd been a victim of gaslighting?

Had her father tried to undermine her recovery from amnesia by lying about not knowing the father of her child?

"I don't claim to understand his motives. But I know I won't be manipulated anymore." She leaned closer and lowered her voice. "Not by him. And not by you."

"I'm trying to protect you." Damon's hands moved to her shoulders, his touch gentle. "And I'm ensuring Lucas's future is secure by introducing Transparent to the market in the most successful way. The company is his legacy."

Some of the anger thrumming through her eased. She understood his point.

"I want that, too." She'd always hoped for Transparent to succeed. She'd been a fan of the concept even before her father had gotten involved with the company. Now, there was far more riding on Damon's public launch, since Lucas would one day inherit whatever his father built.

"Do you?" He let the question hang between them for a moment. "Because if you want the business to succeed in spite of your father, I would appreciate it if you would share your notes. I need to know how much inside information he has."

"I'll do it." She bit her lip, hating being torn between someone she'd felt loyalty toward for the last twenty-plus years of her life and the man she'd married. "If you can tell me how it makes any sense for Dad to sabotage a business that he has an enormous stake in."

"I think revenge has become more important to him than walking away with a profit this time. Especially when he has investments in plenty of other lucrative ventures."

He let go of her shoulders, so that it was only his powerful words that kept her close to him.

"You think he wants revenge enough to ruin his own grandson's future?" She didn't want it to be true. But she couldn't deny all the ways her father's actions had hurt her in the past year.

"Lucas is a McNeill now." Damon straightened. "He might not feel any loyalty to our son."

But she knew for certain Damon would protect their child no matter what. Even if he didn't love her.

"Very well." She nodded, her mind made up. "I'll send you all of my research. Everything that I shared with my father."

# Eight

Damon hated that Caroline was under such tremendous stress. Thank goodness she'd agreed to his idea for a break from it all, a chance to unwind and let the pieces of life slide back into place.

"I didn't think sledding was possible in New York City," Caroline called to him as they crossed Fifth Avenue the next morning, a bodyguard trailing them.

Her cheeks were pink from the cold, her brown eyes bright as they trudged the snowy path already worn from early morning visitors to the park. She wore black ski pants and a bright aquamarine parka with a pair of insulated boots left behind by another guest of his grandfather's. The maids had produced the clothes within minutes of his asking about winter gear. Caroline had brought her own gloves and a white knit hat for the trip, so she'd been well equipped for the outing he'd suggested. He wanted to smooth things over between them after the talk about her father last night.

While she'd complied with his request and sent him the files he'd asked for via email before midnight, Damon had sensed that she was upset. No doubt, she wished things had turned out differently in regard to her father. But in time, she would have to see that Stephan Degraff was far more ruthless than she knew.

"It's the City that Never Sleeps, not the City that Never Plays." Damon juggled the brightly colored inflatable tube under his arm, an item he'd had specially shipped from a local seller capitalizing on the snowstorm. He hoped his own son would one day be as industrious as the teen who'd showed up at the mansion this morning on a fat-tire mountain bike, five more sleds strapped to a wagon on the back.

"But are there hills?" Her gaze swept the bright terrain where a flood of early risers built snowmen along the park paths.

"Seriously?" He draped his free arm around her shoulders to steer her where he wanted to go. "You didn't ever leave your office while you lived here?"

She gave him a sheepish grin and he was glad he'd come up with the sledding idea. He hadn't enjoyed needling her about her father last night. More than anything, he wanted to start their relationship over and cement things between them as a couple. But he had a duty to protect his investment at Transparent, too, for investors but also for his family's financial security. With the public launch around the corner, he needed to ensure the product was protected from Stephan Degraff.

"I told you, I was very focused on work. I loved my job consulting for entrepreneurs. I would have gladly stayed in that field for years if my father hadn't tapped me to help with his venture capital investments." She pointed to a group of evergreens with boughs weighed down to the ground from the snow. "This is all so pretty."

Damon liked the feel of her under his arm, the scent of her shampoo right through the crocheted wool cap she wore.

"Seems like a good time for you to have some fun." He remembered how easy it was to be with her in Italy on their honeymoon. Not just because they'd been in love and eager to spend every second together. But because simple things made her happy. She was unpretentious despite her family's wealth. She'd counseled struggling women entrepreneurs through her work in the financial industry, helping female business owners win grants, negotiate complicated financial regulations and win more capital backing. Damon had always considered her work history a far cry from her father's business interests even though she'd stepped into Transparent as his representative.

Damon had been impressed by her savvy from the

first day. She'd been helpful without being overbearing. She'd genuinely facilitated his company's move forward.

"I will admit, Lucas appears to be in very good hands." She held up her phone in front of Damon as they passed a vendor selling hot chocolate along with hot pretzels. A small crowd clutched steaming foam cups.

Her nursery app showed the two college grads his grandfather had hired. Lucas sat in a baby bouncer on the floor while one of the young women—Marcie, he thought—danced an impromptu ballet to the classical music playing, using a stuffed elephant as her partner. At the same time, her colleague assembled a baby swing in the middle of the room. Wide-eyed, Lucas kicked happily in his seat.

Damon could rest easy leaving their son behind when Lucas had a second security guard assigned to his safety.

"He certainly seems entertained." They trooped through fresh powder to one side of the path as a troop of kids ran by them, squealing and throwing snowballs. "I asked the caregivers to bring him to the park after we finish sledding. In another hour, the plows will have swept through again and it should be easy to push the stroller on the paths." He could see the crowd at the top of Cedar Hill already. "We'll trade off the sled for a baby and a winter picnic. The girls might enjoy trying out the tube once we're done."

"That sounds great and—oh! Look!" Caroline halted

as they turned a corner and got a good view of Cedar Hill crowded with sledders.

A mish-mosh of music drifted up from competing external speakers on a variety of electronic devices. An eighties tune, pop music and some sort of funky electronica overlapped with squeals and laughter even as the fresh snow muted the sounds to a dull, vibrant hum. Toboggans, plastic saucers and a few pieces of cardboard all carried people down the hillside.

"New York sledding at its finest." He let go of her shoulders to hold up the inflated tube. "Are you ready to set the new land speed record?"

"Very." Caroline tugged her knit hat lower on her ears. "Let's show them how it's done."

He watched a family at the bottom of the hill tip their sled into a snowbank, upending the whole group.

"Have you been sledding before?" He knew she'd spent most of her childhood in southern California, but her father's wealth had probably allowed for ski vacations.

"I've gone tubing behind a boat." She dug a pair of sunglasses out of her pocket and slid them on her nose. "How different can it be?"

She headed toward the highest crest where a few groups of people took turns careening down the hill. Damon took a moment to give their security detail a thumbs-up, letting the guy know they would remain in this location for a while. Then he followed Caroline.

"Seriously? You've never ridden a sleigh down a

hill?" Damon wended his way through a mob of parents supervising smaller children on sleds, following Caroline to where a group of teens filmed one another using an empty refrigerator box for a makeshift snowboard.

"This will be a first." She flashed him a smile and pointed out an available spot for the inner tube.

He laid it in the snow. "Didn't you take the obligatory rich-kid trip to the Alps as a teenager? There must be some sledding hills somewhere in all those mountains."

His own teen years had been marked by his mother's death and the emptiness it left behind. He and his brothers had worked their asses off to make something of the property that had been their legacy, the historic plantation house and land in Martinique. They'd kept a portion for living space and they'd turned the rest into an exclusive corporate retreat and private party facility. The income had helped fund his start-up.

"Any cold-weather trips we took were devoted to ski lessons." Caroline seemed to track the progress of a young woman on a tube similar to theirs, watching as she sped down the hill and no doubt cataloging the technique. "My father considers skiing, tennis and golf the most 'business-friendly' sports that any upwardly mobile executive should know."

"Right. Remind me to brush up before I meet you on the links." It should come as no surprise that Caroline had been groomed to take over the man's business interests from an early age, but it bugged Damon to think that Stephan Degraff couldn't be bothered to let her have any fun as a kid.

Time to remedy that.

"Have any pointers?" She dropped down onto the tube and took a seat in the middle.

"Sure I do." He sat down behind her and straddled her. "Be prepared to get close," he said into her ear through the knit hat.

The feel of her curves nestled against his lap reminded him how very much he wanted to visit her bed again. And the ski pants she wore were sexy as hell. He resisted the urge to hug her hips with his thighs—if only for a moment.

"Um. Duly noted." She reached over his knees to grip the handles on either side of the tube. "How do we get going?"

Damon already had his hands planted on the snow behind them. "When we get better at it, I'll get a running start and hop on. But for now, we'll just focus on getting down the hill."

"No land speed record this trip." She nodded. "Got it."

"Ready?" Planting his gloved fingers deeper in the snow, he did something similar to crunches with the tube, letting the sled slide up and down on the slight incline as a warm-up. He flexed his arms and damned if he didn't find himself hugging her hips with his thighs.

It did help him move the sled. The fact that he enjoyed it mightily was a bonus.

"Ready!" She leaned forward, her skiing skills clearly paying off as she pointed them in the right direction on the slope while Damon pushed off with one last shove.

Their combined weight helped them to gain momentum. The inner tube was the perfect choice for the soft conditions. Snow sprayed up from either side, dotting their faces and covering their legs. Caroline whooped with joy as they passed a teenager on a thin plastic sled. With her competitive nature, she clearly loved the thrill of it.

They were almost at the end of the run when they hit an icy patch and picked up speed, spinning sideways and out of control. Tipping precariously, Damon let go of the handles to hold on to Caroline so he took the brunt of the fall. They ended up in the same snowbank as the family he'd watched earlier.

A cloud of snow dusted up from their landing. His shoulder was buried deepest, with Caroline's spine curved against his stomach. Her hips still nestled against his.

"Are you okay?" He shifted his leg off hers.

She shook gently against him.

"Caroline?" A moment of panic punched him in the chest. Had she gotten hurt?

He shouldn't move her if she'd landed badly...

But then, she straightened up on her own, laughter wracking her slender form. Her cap was perched cockeyed on her head, her one cheek red from being pressed in the snow. A crust of icy flakes covered her collar and the side of her hat.

Even her glasses were crooked.

"That was the best!" she managed between laughs that—in his defense—sounded a lot like sobs.

"You scared me." He slumped back against the snow-bank while a sled full of little kids tumbled out a few feet away from them.

Four of them were on their feet almost before they'd finished falling, charging back up the hill on short legs while the youngest of the group screeched at the others to wait for her.

"I didn't mean to frighten you." Caroline pulled the glasses off along with the hat. "My favorite part was the out-of-control three-sixties we were doing at the end."

"You're a madwoman, that's why," he said dryly, his heartbeat only just now slowing back down after the nanosecond when he was convinced she'd broken her neck.

"I mean it. I loved it." She shoved the glasses inside her inner coat pocket. "Let's do it again."

He watched her shove to her feet to dust off the excess snow and a little more of his tension melted away. Because not only was she safe, but she was also having fun.

That put him one step closer to his goal of winning her back this week. Before he removed her father from his business and their lives.

* * *

Caroline's legs were sore from climbing the hill again and again by the time Marcie and Dana arrived with the baby carriage and a picnic hamper on an old-fashioned sled with red metal runners. She noticed the careful eye Lucas's bodyguard kept on the trio, as did the security guard who had trailed her and Damon all day. An inconvenience, perhaps, but it gave her peace of mind. The two young women traded the baby and the picnic provisions for the inner tube, promising to meet them back at the McNeill home in two hours in case they were needed.

Inside the carriage—a fancy stroller with multiple settings for pushing a baby—Lucas was dressed in a tiny winter papoose with a hood. The outfit looked like a dark, insulated bag with a zipper up the front, leaving plenty of room for his legs to kick freely inside. The hood tied with a ribbon under his chin and had tiny dark ears sewn on top, making him resemble an elfin mouse. Or maybe a mousy elf.

Whatever it was, he looked adorable with his bright blue eyes and gummy smile. A reflex smile, according to the baby books she'd read, but so cute nonetheless.

"Are you still up for a winter picnic?" Damon asked, propping his aviators on top of his head.

He practically oozed sex appeal in his dark jeans, red flannel shirt and insulated gray vest. It was West Coast grunge meets New York style. His boots and hiking socks were as snow-covered as hers, but despite the cold, he'd unfastened his vest an hour ago, impervious to the chill in the air now that the sun was shining brightly.

"I'm game." She pointed toward a quieter section of the huge park, away from the hill that had gotten far more crowded since they'd first arrived. "I hope there's plenty of food in there since I've worked up a major appetite."

Damon pulled the sled toward where she pointed. The snow had settled and packed down a bit, making the trekking easier. The baby carriage had rugged wheels, making it easy to handle, if a bit slow. The noise receded the farther they got from the sledding.

"You think Lucas will be okay? It's not too cold for him?" Reaching into the carriage, Damon brushed a knuckle along the baby's cheek.

"Not at all. I'm glad he's getting some fresh air after all the travel yesterday." She noticed that only one security guard trailed them now that they'd reunited with their son. The other guy must have returned to the town house until his next shift.

"The outfit is very cool." Damon gave a light tug on one dark mouse ear. "You think he's a bear?"

"A bear?" She tilted her head sideways. "I thought it was a mouse papoose."

"McNeills are not mice," he announced definitively.

"Why am I not surprised?" She spotted a clearing in a thicket of trees off the path where the snow wasn't quite as deep. "How about over there?"

"Good eyes." Damon steered the sleigh in that direction. "Do you want to switch and have me push the carriage?"

"I've got it." The mild strain in her arms felt pleasant after months of being inactive. "I'm really looking forward to getting back in shape after the pregnancy."

"You look beautiful." He rested his hand lightly on the middle of her back before dropping a kiss on her hair.

"Thank you." His words warmed her as much as the touch. "But it will be nice to build up more endurance again. I guess it's a good thing babies aren't mobile for the first months."

"I'm here to help you," he reminded her as they reached the clearing. He lifted the picnic hamper and slid out a folded blanket. "I hope you remember you're not in this alone anymore."

He shook out the waterproof blanket on the snow—plastic on one side, wool plaid on the other. She watched him line up the sled at one end of the blanket before he knelt in the snow to open the picnic hamper. All the while, Caroline rocked the carriage gently, tilting it back and forth. Thankfully, their bodyguard sat outside the trees, keeping an eye on the hill below to make sure no one intruded on their space. She didn't feel "watched," per se, although she felt certain the guy kept an eye on them somehow. The team Damon hired seemed very skilled at maintaining a discreet presence.

"I know that I'm not alone any longer, and I'm glad

for that." She debated lifting Lucas out of the baby carrier, but then changed her mind, putting the brakes on the contraption and facing the carrier toward the blanket so they could keep an eye on him.

"Are you ready for the winter picnic to end all picnics?" Damon asked, waiting to open the picnic basket until he had her attention.

He shoved his gloves into the pockets of his vest. His dark hair had a few fresh snowflakes coating the top where he must have brushed against one of the evergreen boughs.

"Do you know what's in there?" She peeled off her own gloves, ready to eat. "I can't imagine what a winter picnic entails, so my expectations are fairly low."

"I packed this myself. And believe me, my expectations run permanently high." He tipped open the lid with a flourish. "I present to you, the Post-Sledding Woodland Feast."

Caroline felt her eyes go wide. Crammed inside the huge basket were two brightly colored thermoses and insulated mugs, a red-and-white-checkered tablecloth, a wooden cheeseboard with fresh fruits and cloth-covered cheeses, a tray of shrimp on ice, a stack of Sternos and a lighter, a bag of huge, homemade-looking marshmallows, a tin of graham crackers, chocolate-covered strawberries...

"And champagne!" Her gaze finally reached a bottle of a highly recognizable brand of bubbly inside a champagne bucket. "Is that even legal?" She glanced around, half expecting a park ranger to issue a citation.

"Alcohol in the park is regulated, but not prohibited, so no one will bother us unless we start causing trouble." Grinning, he gestured for her to have a seat on the blanket. "Get comfortable and I'll serve us."

She did as he asked, her eyes still on the stuffed hamper.

"You packed this?" It was a feat of engineering, the way everything was stacked and prepped.

"The technical mind is good for more than designing software, you know." He pulled out fondue sticks and set them beside the Sterno cans so they could toast their own marshmallows. "And under the champagne is a bottle of whiskey if you'd rather doctor up the hot chocolate." He produced a smaller basket with airline-sized bottles of Jameson and Baileys, plus a variety of add-in flavors from vanilla and almond to butterscotch.

"You have outdone yourself." She glanced up into the carriage to check on Lucas. Surrounded by trees on three sides, their picnic spot felt safe and surprisingly private considering the view of the mayhem near Cedar Hill and the row of emerging snowmen lining the biggest walking trail less than fifty yards away.

"I will admit, it's been hell keeping a lid on the surprise all day." He found two small hurricane lanterns and placed candles inside them even though the sun still shone brightly outside. Then, he uncapped one of the containers of cocoa and poured her a mugful. "Here. You can add what you like while I work on the seating."

He scrambled around to the back of the blanket where he used one arm to scoop a pile of snow under the edge of the wool plaid. It took her a moment to understand why he wanted a big lump of snow under the spot where she was sitting. But then he covered it up again, packing the pile into a U-shaped curve to create a support for her back.

"Genius," she announced, settling into the snow seat with her mug of hot chocolate, the picnic spread out at her feet. "It really is the picnic to end all picnics."

"I'll drink to that." Damon poured his own hot chocolate and settled on the blanket beside her. "Here's to our first real day as a family."

She met his blue gaze, his eyes all the more crystalline in the bright sun. He'd taken considerable time and trouble to make the day perfect for her, and Lucas, too. While she'd been sleeping late to catch up on rest, he'd been ordering a special sled and packing the perfect picnic.

"To family," she echoed, softly clanking her pewter cup to his.

Tipping the drink to her lips, she savored the complex swirl of flavors. She hadn't added much alcohol, just enough to give a pleasant jolt of warmth on the way down. The almond and vanilla notes were especially good, and the melting homemade marshmallow she'd set on top was a gooey bonus.

She was about to compliment the first beverage course, but when she turned to him again, she felt a flash of heat from the simmering look he gave her. His mug remained untouched, his attention fixed on her mouth.

He was very still.

"What?" Self-conscious, she set her cup aside in the snow. "I have marshmallow all over my face, don't I?"

Her hand went to her nose, but Damon caught it. He'd set his own drink aside, too, freeing his hands.

"Let me." He canted closer, his focus shifting to her eyes.

The heat ratcheted up so much it was a wonder they weren't melting snow.

She could feel her heartbeat quicken, the answering spark she'd always experienced with this man. Time and distance hadn't broken it. Even forgetting him completely for weeks on end hadn't erased the response she had to him.

By the time his mouth brushed hers, she had somehow crept closer to him, her hands slipping under the vest he wore to rest on the flannel shirt over his chest. His heart sped quicker, its rhythm synchronized with hers in a dance she remembered all too well.

He tasted like whiskey, a straight shot that imparted a stronger burn than any drink. She let the feel of his kiss fill her whole body, the nerve endings coming to life from the roots of her hair to the most intimate heart of her being. His tongue coaxed and toyed with hers, slowly at first. Then harder. More demanding.

Her pulse pounded faster. She breathed in the sandalwood of his aftershave and fresh pine all around them, her senses all attuned to the pleasure to come.

Until Damon slowed the kiss again.

Stopped.

Pulled back just a fraction of an inch.

Caroline's fingers clutched at his shirt, holding him. Wanting him.

It took a long moment for her to return to the moment and the picnic. The feast he'd carefully planned for her. The bodyguard protecting them, who'd no doubt gotten an eyeful. Dragging in gulps of cold air, she hoped the winter chill would put out some of the fire inside. She forced her fingers to unclench from where she gripped his shirt. Thank goodness they were in a public park with a baby in the carriage beside them or she might have toppled him onto his back and lost herself in the feel of him.

"You had a little bit of marshmallow," he explained belatedly, reaching up to graze her upper lip with his thumb. "Right here."

Even now, his touch sparked a powerful need.

"Then I'll have to be careful with my next taste." She picked up her mug for another drink, grateful for something else to focus on besides Damon's touch. The way he looked at her.

"No need," he assured her, reaching toward the sled

full of food to drag the cheese board closer. "The pleasure was all mine."

His wolfish grin was very male. And even as he goaded her, she knew her defenses would never hold if he kissed her again.

# Nine

After sledding and a picnic, Damon thought Caroline seemed more relaxed. They'd made a plan for dinner in front of the fire in her suite, a location he didn't even have to lobby for since she wanted to stay close to Lucas and his room was on the same floor as hers. Her bedroom had a sitting room with a table, and she'd suggested it would be more relaxing to have a simple meal up there as opposed to the formal dining space.

That she *wanted* to unwind around him seemed like a personal victory.

He pushed the baby's carriage across Fifth Avenue while the bodyguard who accompanied them pulled the sled with the picnic hamper and leftovers. Damon hadn't wanted Caroline to overexert herself, and it had been a busy day already.

"So I'm going to feed Lucas while you relax for a little while." He reminded her of the plan as they approached the huge town house. "Just text me when you're ready for dinner and I'll have it brought up."

"Thank you." She hugged her arms around herself. The temperature was dropping now that the sun had dipped low on the horizon. "It was fun getting outdoors today. It made me realize how long I've been cooped up inside, between caring for Lucas and being sick."

Damon didn't remind her that she'd been a prisoner in her father's home as much as she had been in Mexico. He hoped with time she would comprehend the depth of her father's betrayal. Did she understand that Damon would never allow Lucas to be near Stephan Degraff again?

"Speaking of which, I confirmed an appointment with a highly respected local therapist for you tomorrow." He unlocked the door to the town house, unwilling to bother the staff inside. Besides, they had enough witnesses to private conversations with the security lurking behind them. "Maybe she'll have new ideas for helping you recover your memories and your health."

If Caroline recovered her full memory, it would go a long way in convincing her to stay away from her father. Assuming, of course, she was genuinely committed to starting this marriage over. He had at least ruled out his concern that she might be conspiring against him with her father. Damon believed she was invested in discovering the truth.

"Thank you." She stepped inside while he held the door for her. "I'd like that."

He barely had time to savor that small triumph when the bodyguard who'd been stationed at the house stalked into the foyer, a paper in hand.

This one was Wade, he recalled. The guy had an impressive scar on the side of his neck and a don't-mess-with-me demeanor that Damon appreciated in a protector.

"Is everything all right?" Damon's eyes darted to Lucas and Caroline, and he reassured himself they were still right there with him. He reached into the baby carriage to lift his son from the seat so he could cradle him in his arms.

Behind him, Caroline slid off her boots and left them on a mat to one side of the entry. She padded closer in stocking feet as she unzipped her bright parka.

"There's been no activity to report here," Wade assured him. "But it's a different story back at the Los Altos Hills house." He passed Damon the paper while Caroline stood by him to peer over his shoulder. "The security cameras caught this guy on film shortly before he asked one of the groundskeepers if you were in residence. He took off without giving his name."

"It's the fisherman who rescued me." Caroline's arm brushed against his as she tilted the photo toward her for a better view. "I'm sure of it."

It damn well couldn't be a coincidence.

"This guy?" Damon gave the black-and-white print-out to her so she could look more closely. "This is the same man who pulled you out of the water off the coast in Mexico?"

"Yes." She nodded. "But I don't understand why, that is, how he would find me. Unless—" She went very still. "Do you think he found out something about who kidnapped me? Or where I was being held?"

The bodyguard appeared ready to offer more information, but Damon held up a hand to delay his input, wanting to hear what conclusions Caroline reached on her own. If she was close to a breakthrough with her memories, he didn't want to stifle it.

When Caroline's dark eyes met his, he tried to help her think through the possibility she'd suggested.

"It seems unlikely a fisherman living south of the border would make a trip to the US to find you." He articulated what she had to be thinking already. "Furthermore, you didn't remember me at the time, let alone your married name. So he wouldn't know to look for you at the Los Altos Hills house."

Her face paled. She shook her head.

"You think he works for my father." She thrust the photo back at Damon and spun away, pressing the heels of her hands against her closed eyes. "That he worked for my father even then. Which would mean he didn't save me at all. He just acted out another part of some elaborate drama my father created to keep us apart?"

Straightening, she relaxed her arms and opened her eyes. "Why would he ever do that? He's not a madman, Damon. He's just—"

She couldn't quite fill in that blank.

Damon resisted the urge to do so himself, since he had a wealth of names to label the bastard, but none of them would line up with whatever fairy tale Caroline concocted in her mind to account for her father's behavior. One day, she would be able to see her father's actions for what they were—calculated, self-serving and, yes, unbalanced.

It was bad enough Stephan had thwarted an investigation of Caroline's disappearance. If it turned out that he had masterminded her kidnapping? He was going to prison, no question.

"What else were you able to find out about him?" Damon asked, turning back toward Wade.

As much as Damon wanted to comfort his wife, her safety came first. He lifted Lucas higher against his chest, kissing the baby's downy head while the little boy stretched sleepily.

"His name is Theo Bastien." The bodyguard pulled out a phone and seemed to read from his notes. "He's a French-Canadian transplant who moved to Vancouver two years ago, when his employment history shows he started as a chauffeur and groundskeeper for Stephan Degraff, who keeps a rental home there and visits frequently."

At Caroline's muffled cry, Damon interrupted the

report. "Whatever you need to make sure the properties are both protected, it's yours. For now, I'd like a copy of the information to go to Officer Downey at the Los Altos Hills police department."

"We've already called it in," Wade assured him. "The police still haven't been able to locate Degraff to interview him."

"Thank you." Damon dismissed him with a nod and waved over the head housekeeper waiting on the periphery of the huge foyer. The McNeill mansion had no lack of personal servants. "Would you find Marcie and let her know Lucas is ready for a bottle? I'm going upstairs with my wife and we'll take dinner in her suite in two hours."

"Of course." The woman nodded, her face a professional mask as she accepted the squirming six-week-old, easily cradling him against her starched gray livery. "Your security team suggested we don't open the door to anyone but uniformed police officers or McNeill family members." She lifted a dark eyebrow, seeking confirmation.

"Correct." Damon tightened his hold on Caroline, feeling her trembling right through her warm winter clothes. "And please be as vigilant at the service entrance. No delivery people past the gates."

"Certainly. I'll remind Marcie to stay in the nursery where you can monitor the little one." The woman spared a brief smile for the wriggling baby before turning on one quiet heel and disappearing down the hallway that led to the service elevator, the bodyguard behind her.

With Lucas cared for and the home well-guarded, Damon could turn his attention to Caroline. His plans for winning her back tonight would have to be deferred after the devastating revelations she was still trying to process. He steered her toward the elevator, hugging her close to his side.

A few minutes later, Caroline swayed on her feet inside the suite's lavish dressing room, her brain pinging with too many worries, thoughts and fears to name them all.

Could her father really have arranged to have her kidnapped? Her head throbbed with as much pain as her heart to think about that while she searched for a clean tee and pajama pants—comfort clothes. It seemed easier to believe she'd walked out on her husband than that her father would be so cruelly calculating.

People ended relationships all the time, after all. And she had been arguing with Damon when she was in London before she flew back to the Los Altos Hills house. What if the holes in her memory had steered her all wrong? What if she hadn't been kidnapped? Maybe she'd asked for her father's help in walking away from the marriage…

That scenario made her head hurt less, but her heart protested just as much. She had been wildly in love with her husband, and no amount of secrets or betrayals could dim that fact. Stepping into warm blue flannel pj pants, she reminded herself that she'd seen evidence of her happiness in those honeymoon photos. The joy in the pictures couldn't be faked.

She ran a brush through her hair and tapped her phone to pull up the video feed of Lucas in the nursery. The baby curled against Marcie while the young woman sat with him in a rocker, the lights dim. The fresh air had tired them all out today.

Stepping out of the dressing room, she found Damon in front of the fireplace in the small sitting room. He'd rearranged the furniture a little so the gray couch was closer to the hearth where he'd built a real fire from the supply of logs in a wrought iron grate. An elaborate white mantelpiece was decorated with a relief sculpture of figures in ball gowns beside a carriage, surrounded by servants with torches lighting the way.

Pivoting from the grate with a poker in his hand, Damon watched her move toward him.

"I just wanted to stay long enough to build a fire and make sure you are okay."

The authenticity in his voice washed over her. He truly was a kind and thoughtful man underneath the intense, work-driven exterior. If Damon had done nothing wrong in all this, and her father bore the full brunt of the blame for what happened to her, she couldn't begin to imagine how hurt her husband must have been at her disappearance.

He had missed out on so much by not being a part

of Lucas's birth. And if she didn't handle things well moving forward, if she couldn't sort through what had happened and recover some additional memories, she ran the risk of hurting him all the more. Yet she ached everywhere whenever she tried to force herself to remember.

"It causes physical pain to think about my father…" She couldn't even finish the sentence. Her eyes stung, but that pain was minor in comparison to how her head throbbed.

"Then don't think about it." He set aside the wrought iron poker and rose to meet her. He laid his hands on the part of her upper arms exposed by her tee. "Are you warm enough in this?"

"Kind of." She wasn't. "Actually, I don't think there are enough sweaters to ward off the sort of chill I'm feeling anyhow."

"Come and sit." He tugged her phone from her hand and propped it on the arm of the sofa before gently pushing her onto the seat cushion directly opposite the blaze in the hearth. "I'll get you a blanket."

Drawing her feet up underneath her, she double-checked that she could still see the nursery video feed. Marcie had moved the camera so that it was closer to the crib, where Lucas now slept with his favorite dinosaur blanket.

"Here you go." Damon returned with a snowy white quilt for her, and he draped it around her so that it covered all of her from the neck down.

"Thank you." She caught at his hand where he'd tucked the quilt closer to her chin. "Lucas is already sleeping if you want to stay with me a little while longer."

She needed him, ached to have his arms around her to help bear a burden she still couldn't wrap her brain around. She could not hurt this man any more than she already had.

"I don't want to keep you from your rest." He leaned closer to her, stroking a thumb over the back of her hand. "I know you must be exhausted."

"I'll never sleep with so much on my mind." She snaked a hand out from the blanket and gripped his arm, drawing him toward her on the sofa. "Please."

They could find comfort in a physical connection, at least. She would not deny them that.

"I know you don't want to think the worst of him." He dropped onto the cushion beside her. He'd taken off the vest and flannel he'd worn for sledding, leaving just his gray tee between her hands and his warm chest as she nestled closer to lay her head on his shoulder.

"He's my father. My only living parent." She bit her lip as soon as she said it, knowing he didn't have a relationship at all with his remaining parent. "Didn't it hurt sometimes when you first made the decision to cut your father out of your life, even knowing he hadn't treated your mother fairly?"

She stared into the flames in the hearth, which provided the only light in the room now that the sun had fully set for the evening. She felt the steady thrum of Damon's heart beneath her ear. He slid his arm around her, stroking her hair where it lay on her back.

"I was twelve. It wasn't a decision so much as a fact of life. Dad wasn't coming back and Mom was sick of his pretending he would ever leave his wife to be a part of our family. She made the decision, not me."

"But what about later? After your mother passed and you could have contacted your father again?" she prodded, honestly needing any guidance she could get to figure out how to excise a parent from her life. "I mean, how can you go from loving someone to deciding not to love them anymore?"

Her eyes stung when she spoke the words aloud. Because that was where things stood for her now. She'd have to find a way to un-love someone who didn't have her best interests at heart. But after a lifetime of looking up to her dad, that wasn't going to come easily.

"By the time my mother died, it wasn't hard to hate my father. We blamed him for not being there to help her through the chemo." His voice was rough and he cleared his throat. "For forcing her to move halfway across the globe far from her family. Hell, we blamed him for everything."

"But it was your mother's idea to move far away, right? He never knew she had cancer." She tried to remember the bits that he'd shared with her long ago about his family. He wasn't a man who willingly shared much personal information.

Damon McNeill might be a tech genius and an ambitious businessman she admired, but he kept his emotions in check and his past closely guarded.

"My brothers and I didn't see it that way. My father was a serial cheater with a whole other family. It was Liam's fault that Mom felt like she had no options. I believe she secretly hoped that a drastic move might shake up her lover and force him to realize he loved her." His shoulder lifted a fraction beneath her cheek. A subtle shrug. "When it didn't work, she lost some of her joy. Her will to live. The cancer found a victim without much fight left."

Caroline kissed his chest, rubbing her cheek against him there. "I'm so sorry you lost her at such a young age." She lifted her head, straightening so she could see him. "No wonder you didn't want to see your father afterward. I don't really want to see mine, either. Although I guess a part of me still wants to just ask him why?"

The fire popped and crackled in the hearth, the flames leaping higher as a windy gust blew over the chimney, making a whooshing sound. The shifting of logs stirred the scent of wood smoke.

"Maybe one day you'll be able to. But until we can be sure you're not in danger around him—and that you're not putting Lucas in danger—you'll have to settle for whatever answers the police can shake loose from this investigation." Damon's response was careful. Considered.

And she could read between the lines enough to know he didn't ever want her to have anything to do with Stephan Degraff again. But what about her brothers who were still in his legal care? She couldn't simply write them off. Or worse, leave them in the custody of a man who might not have their best interests at heart.

Wouldn't she need to maintain some kind of dialogue with her family because of them?

"I'm hoping the police find him soon." There had been no news today outside of the report from the security guard about the inquiry at the Los Altos Hills house. "He'll have to put in an appearance at the Transparent investors meeting this week, won't he?"

She felt Damon's shoulders tense. His hand stilled on her back.

"If he's going to follow through on his plans to oust me from the CEO position, yes." The muscle under one eye ticked, and he seemed to weigh the merit of saying anything more. Finally, he let out a gusty breath. "I realize you have a stake in this business, Caroline, but considering all you've been through, I'm hoping you don't feel the need to be a part of a contentious board meeting."

"You're right I have a stake in Transparent. And I will have a lot of guilt and responsibility to bear if my father succeeds in railroading you out of the business before the launch." She'd convinced her dad to invest heavily in the company because she believed in Damon. Now, her husband could be pressured into vacating his seat if Stephan convinced other investors that they would make money with a more seasoned CEO at the helm.

A bloodless, professional executive who took a huge salary to mine the business's assets for the sake of a fatter bottom line.

"I won't let that happen." Damon gripped both ends of the blanket around her shoulders. "Thanks to the notes you shared with me last night—all your research into the business—I know what Stephan knows. That gives me an edge."

Her head throbbed again as she remembered happier days with her father. He'd been so proud when she'd been accepted into a prestigious business program for her master's. She had always thought of him as her biggest champion. What happened to that man?

But her business know-how—the degree and experience her father had helped give her—provided her with unique insight into the situation now. "You won't have enough of an advantage to regain control. His share is significant, Damon. Even if he can't convince other investors to remove you, he's not going away. He added a right of first refusal clause into your initial contract with him so he could invest more in Transparent."

Stephan Degraff had put himself on a track to rule the company with that restrictive clause.

Yet Damon tipped his chin up, a gleam in those deep blue eyes.

"The McNeills can afford to buy him out."

The realization of his calculated move shouldn't have surprised her. Maybe if she wasn't recovering from amnesia and childbirth, she would have seen it sooner.

"Of course." Understanding dawned more fully. "So you're not in New York City to join the family fold. You came here purely for business reasons."

"And safety purposes. I wanted to get you and Lucas out of Los Altos Hills." He smoothed his fingers over the embroidery on the edge of the quilt, and no matter how frustrated she felt that he'd kept this secret from her, she still wished his hands were on her instead of the blanket.

The picnic and sledding had eroded her defenses. She wanted the comfort of his arms, his kisses that made her forget everything but him.

"So you're not interested in being a part of McNeill Resorts? Inheriting the McNeill legacy?" She took some small comfort that at least he hadn't married her to fulfill the requirements of Malcolm McNeill's will the way she'd once feared.

"Transparent is the only legacy our son needs. And it's one I built with you at my side." The heat in his eyes, the fierceness of the words, convinced her.

He might have hidden his deeper motive for traveling to New York, but perhaps he'd only wanted to shield her from more of her father's schemes. She absolutely believed Damon was the kind of man who would want to build a corporate empire all his own—something apart from his wealthy father and grandfather. She understood that desire a little too well. With the benefit of hindsight, she sure wished she'd put more separation between her work and her dad's company.

But right now, she didn't want to look backward.

"Then you really want us to be a team again." She plucked Damon's hand from where he played with the quilt binding, holding it between hers. "We would need to be stronger than we were before all this happened." She was a different woman now. A mother.

And things were far more complicated.

He watched her with an almost predatory stillness.

"I thought I made that clear the night I put your rings back where they belong." He used his free hand to lift her left one to his mouth.

He kissed her ring finger just below the wedding band set. The feel of his lips on her skin incited awareness. Promised pleasure. And yes, added to her fears about where all this was heading.

She worried about the board meeting. Her memory. Their future. But for now…she could savor this moment with him. This one thing they had that had always been perfect.

"You said you wanted us to start over." She remembered that night so clearly. His invitation had mesmerized her into an explosive kiss. "That you wanted us to be a couple again."

"I do." His fingers aligned with hers before he pivoted his palm a few degrees, bending his fingers into the spaces between hers. An act suddenly intimate.

He stole her breath.

She had to lick her lips to speak again, her mouth gone dry. "Then I think it's time we lived up to those words."

# Ten

There had been a time in his relationship with Caroline where those words would have scorched Damon's skin, launching a blistering encounter against the back of a door, the top of a desk, or anywhere else they happened to be. They'd spent weeks on their honeymoon indulging every erotic impulse, driving each other crazy over expensive dinners, only to race back to the hotel before dessert so they could peel one another's clothes off.

But he couldn't afford to let that instinct take over quite yet. Not when his future—his family—hung in the balance of this marriage.

"What about your health?" He hadn't talked to her about her visits with the obstetrician. They'd spoken about the amnesia. About Lucas's well-being after the way Caroline had been drugged while pregnant. "Are you sure it's safe for you? So soon after giving birth?"

He had to grit out the words, doing his damnedest to ignore the blaze of heat climbing his back, the need for her stronger than ever after so long apart.

"My doctor in Vancouver said I could resume all normal activity." She walked her fingers up his forearm, a teasing invitation to touch her that worked so well he felt the first hint of sweat bead along his shoulders.

"How can you be certain that means—"

"I asked," she interrupted, a sure sign she was feeling the effects of holding back every bit as much as him. "Point blank."

Her gaze dipped to his mouth.

*Yeah. Game over.*

He speared a hand through her long, silky hair, angling her head for his kiss. Her quick intake of air caused her breasts to brush against his chest, that sexy gasp of surprise only fueling his fire.

She tasted like marshmallow and strawberries, her lips soft and yielding. The kiss sealed them, drawing her body closer to wrap all over his. He didn't know if he did that, or if somehow she did, but the blanket fell away as her breasts pressed to his chest, the subtle curves molding against him. Even through their two tees and her bra, he could feel the tight points of her response, which echoed the same fiery desire that had been riding him for days.

Consumed with the need to see her, feel her,

he broke the kiss enough to scrape aside the cotton V-neck, to shove away the lace of the bra enough to taste one rosy-pink peak.

Her fingers curved along his shoulders, scraping lightly as her head fell back. Her spine arched, giving him more access, her throaty moan vibrating on a sizzling frequency he could feel like a physical stroke up his sex.

He unclasped the hook in the front, freeing more of her. With impatient hands, he skimmed the clothes up and off of her, baring her to his view in the firelight. One tousled strand of honey-gold hair curled down her neck to land between her breasts. Her body was different— the curves fuller, the tips darker—than he remembered. And even more tempting.

With that visual reminder, he took a deep breath. Told himself to be careful with her no matter how much they both wanted this.

"Let me take you to bed." He slipped one arm beneath her and another around her shoulders. "We should go slow. And you should be comfortable."

He said it to himself as much as her. A stern reminder to the possessive hormones urging him for more. Now. Faster.

For her, he would shut that voice up.

"I dreamed of you all the time." She whispered the words while he cradled her against his chest, scooping up her phone to bring with them before carrying her from the sitting room to the sleeping area of the suite. "Before they drugged me too much to remember. I dreamed about you holding me, just like this."

She rubbed her cheek against him, her eyes closing in a sweep of dark lashes. He hated that he hadn't been there for her when she needed him. When she'd been frightened, and alone, and expecting his baby.

He kissed the top of her head, pausing at the edge of the king-size poster bed. Holding her steady, he used two fingers to sweep back the snowy white duvet and lay her on the sheets, resting her head on the thick down pillow. He tugged off his shirt and his dark denim pants before sliding into bed beside her.

"It's not a dream anymore." He trailed his fingers down her cheek to tip her chin up. "We're together now. And I'll never let anything happen to you again."

A small smile curved her lips and she sidled closer to him, her hands smoothing down his chest, slowing at his waist.

"I don't want a bodyguard forever." She kissed his shoulder, her tongue darting out to flick along the spot she kissed. "I'd settle for you making the sexy parts of my dreams come true."

He stilled her questing hand and flipped her to her back.

"I'm being careful with you, Caroline." He splayed his hand on her bare stomach, his fingers spanning narrow hips to cover the place where she'd carried his son. "At least this first time."

"I'm not fragile." She burrowed her hand beneath

his to untie the drawstring on her pajama pants. She used the loosened ribbons to snake along his arm. "If there's one thing this year has taught me, it's that I'm stronger than I knew, Damon McNeill. And I want this." She arched up to kiss him fully on the mouth. "You."

He closed his eyes, a shuddering sigh rushing through him.

"I can fight myself, but I'll be damned if I can fight you, too."

Her smile—full of victory and feminine wisdom— torched the last of his restraint.

Kissing his way down her body, he dragged her cotton pajama pants down and off, admiring the way her skin looked in the glow from the fire across the room. Bronze flickered with shadow along her pale flesh and black lace panties. He hooked a finger in the skinny expanse of elastic on her hip and peeled that last layer away.

Her smile faded a moment before he dipped his head to kiss the dark triangle above her thighs. She shifted her legs, one smooth calf grazing his shoulder. Her skin smelled like roses—a body oil or soap maybe. Everything about her was familiar and yet different, too.

But the way she tasted…perfect. Just like he remembered.

She made tiny, helpless sounds as he kissed her intimately, losing himself in the feel of her slick heat. She twitched and wriggled, her hips rocking for a moment, her back arching. Then, she went utterly still.

He remembered that, too.

He didn't let that slow his pace. He gripped her thighs. Steadied her. She came apart with sweet cries, her fingers gripping the sheets and twisting as the spasms rolled over her. When the last seemed to have its way with her, he tasted his way up her hip. Her stomach.

Caroline was having none of it, though. Her hands were surprisingly strong as she locked onto his arms and tried to pull him higher. He gave in to the wordless demand, prepared to please her thoroughly now that he felt sure she was relaxed. Healed.

And very ready for him.

"You did that on purpose," she accused him breathlessly before she kissed him, attempting to roll on top of him.

"Pleasured you on purpose?" he teased, nipping her shoulder as he let her take charge. "Is that a bad thing?"

"I thought we could…" she reached beneath the covers to peel away his boxers and finished dragging them off his legs with an agile foot "…you know. Find that peak together."

She straddled his thigh while she stroked him. The sexiest wife a man ever called his own.

"Sweetheart." He gripped her narrow waist, molded his hands around her hips. "Your memory really has taken a hit if you don't recall how easily we can get right back to that high point again."

She gave him that smile again. The one he'd once planned to move mountains for.

"You're wicked. But you're right." She shifted her legs, positioned herself above him and took the sweetest revenge imaginable.

Time stopped.

Caroline was sure it did for one protracted moment as she reunited with Damon in the most fundamental way.

The night wrapped around them, everything dark and shadowy except for their bodies in the reflected glow of the hearth. Skin to skin. Heart to heart. She breathed in the scent of her soap and his aftershave. Her shampoo and the fragrant applewood smoke.

Damon's blue eyes locked with hers, communicating things he never shared in words. She couldn't possibly understand him. She knew this much, though. There was no denying their connection. It *had* to mean something. The longing for him. Craving him. Missing him.

In her mind and her heart, that added up to a new hope.

"Caroline." His voice was gruff with unfulfilled desire, reminding her he hadn't reached that finish point he'd already given her.

Gladly, she lost herself all over again, giving in to the feel of his hands on her hips as he guided her higher. Faster.

This was a language they understood. He made her feel beautiful. Sexual. Desirable. And she couldn't possibly get enough of him. She wished time would stop again so they could go on and on this way, relishing every shared breath and sigh. But now, the moments sped faster, driving her toward the inevitable as pleasure twined tight inside her.

Just as he'd predicted.

She tried to slow everything down, but she felt the gallop of Damon's heart, the rush of his need. She had no choice but to hang onto him. To brace herself for…

Sensation gripped her, tossed her in the waves of another heady orgasm that undulated through her again and again. She knew that his completion came at the same time as hers, felt the harsh tensing of his body and heard the guttural shout. Yet she was so lost in what she was feeling, she couldn't even find the will to peel her spent body off of him for long moments afterward.

She simply curled onto his chest, trying to catch her breath, comforted by the rhythm of his heartbeat beneath her ear.

In time, he turned them both sideways, easing her off him to lie next to him in the fading firelight from a blaze that needed stirring. It was early yet. They hadn't even had dinner. But it felt so right to be with him.

Naked. Fulfilled. Happy.

Save for one tiny thought at the back of her brain.

In the past, the aftermath of sex had always been a time for more intimate words. Another sort of connection they'd once enjoyed.

*I love you*, he might have once whispered in her ear, stroking her hair as she fell asleep. Now, the gentle glide of his fingers through the long strands felt strangely...quiet.

Forcefully quiet.

As if there was an effort not to say anything he might regret later.

Sleepily, she opened one eye to peer up at him, trying to gauge his expression. Brow furrowed, he seemed to concentrate on her hair as if the way he combed his fingers through were of monumental importance.

Because he was busy telling himself it didn't matter that he no longer loved her?

Probably she was reading too much into the moment. Even though the sex had been as earth-moving as ever, they were still off in their conversational rhythms. They'd been apart too long.

Caroline hoped that was all there was to it. Because if her husband didn't love her anymore, it didn't matter how beautiful, sexual or desirable he made her feel.

It didn't even matter that they shared a child together, although she would hurt more for Lucas's sake.

No. If Damon didn't love her, no power on earth could make Caroline stay.

# Eleven

Two hours later, Damon cradled Lucas in his arms and stared out into the snowy night through a window that overlooked Central Park to the west. Behind him, Caroline picked at the desserts after the small meal they'd shared in the sitting room of her suite, an informal affair to make it easier to spend time with the baby. His son blinked up at him with wide blue eyes, his expression content. His little face was so familiar now.

With his wife back in his bed, once more committed to being a couple, Damon should share that sense of contentment. Being with Caroline again reminded him that he was in reach of all his goals. Now that his family was secure, he could focus on his company. His son's legacy.

Except something was still off.

He could feel the disconnect between them now no matter that the sex had been so good it had left them nearly delirious, blissed out and languorous in the sheets together long afterward. Something was missing in their marriage. Something they'd had before and hadn't recaptured. He felt the loss all the more for having known her full love. The off-the-charts intimacy hadn't patched the hole left by the lack of trust.

Surely that was the missing piece. Questioning one another, the betrayals and secrets, had left them with a deep uneasiness no matter how hard they worked to be a team. Damned if he knew how to restore that bond.

A brusque knock on the door called him from brooding thoughts. Caroline set down her plate and moved as if to rise.

"I'll get it." He strode to the door, not wanting her disturbed.

He'd seen a marked improvement in her health since they'd been reunited and he didn't want to slow her recovery by stressing her any more. He enjoyed seeing hints of her competitive spirit return. Some of her natural joy.

Wade stood on the other side.

"Sorry to disturb you." The guy's black pants and tee were neatly pressed, but appeared to be off-duty wear, making Damon wonder if there was a problem.

"What's wrong?" Instinctively, he looked past the

guard into the hallway, shifting Lucas to the arm farther from the door.

"You have visitors. We started to run a check on them before we bothered you, but the staff vouched for them. It's your half brother and his wife, Cameron and Maresa McNeill." He flipped his phone screen around for Damon to see.

Sure enough, Damon's doppelganger showed up on the screen—the half brother who looked most like him. "Yeah. We'd better let the family through the door or I'll get booted out of here." He had thought Cameron was going to wait until tomorrow to show, but Damon didn't feel right turning him away when this was his grandfather's house.

Caroline arrived at Damon's side, her silky hair brushing his shirt sleeve as she joined him in time to glance at the photo of his relative.

"Just doing my job." Wade pocketed the phone and nodded an acknowledgment to Caroline. "The housekeeper wanted them to wait in the library, so I sent Joseph to keep a discreet eye on the third floor while they're here."

"Dismiss him, but thank you. We'll go down to them in a few minutes." He closed the door behind the bodyguard, pivoting to face his wife. "I can make your excuses. I'm sure they'll understand—"

"I'm eager to meet them," she surprised him by saying. "I'll just slip into a dress."

"Are you sure?" He would have discouraged her if

Cam hadn't brought along his wife. He could hardly claim this was a brothers-only meeting.

"With my own family disintegrating, Damon, I look forward to connecting with yours." She was already moving toward the dressing room. "You might not care about nurturing a relationship with your grandfather and half brothers, but for Lucas's sake, I would like him to have the chance to be part of a bigger family."

Was that a positive sign? Maybe if Caroline felt more deeply connected to the rest of his relatives, he could finally feel like they were a team again. A real couple.

United.

"Very well. If you don't mind, I'll take Lucas to the nursery and go down now to greet them. Come downstairs whenever you're ready."

"Thank you." She retreated into the dressing area.

No doubt she wanted to hurry along her preparations. That's probably why she'd seemed flustered.

But as he departed the bedroom suite where they'd renewed their marriage, he couldn't shake the sense that Caroline was still holding something back from him. Was she actively keeping secrets from him?

Or did she simply fear—as he did—that her unrecovered memories might reveal deeper rifts in their marriage than he'd ever be able to fix?

Logically, Caroline understood that integrating herself into the McNeill family wouldn't magically make her feel like a real McNeill again.

But knowing as much didn't stop her from throwing herself wholeheartedly into a private conversation with her breathtakingly beautiful sister-in-law as they had after dinner drinks in the third-floor library. Caroline acknowledged that she'd been too isolated by her father. Even during her time working in New York, away from him, she hadn't strayed far from her office. Maybe if she'd surrounded herself with a larger network, she wouldn't have been so susceptible to his control. She would make sure her son had more influences in his life.

Now, she and Maresa were able to speak privately on the couch while Damon and Cameron conversed on the other side of room behind the huge desk that dominated one side of the library.

"So your brother is really happy here?" Caroline asked, sitting beside Maresa McNeill on a huge leather sofa in the mahogany-paneled room surrounded by books and beautiful, antique, Chinese lacquer panels hung on the walls between the windows.

There was a faint scent of leather and wood smoke from yet another fireplace. Had Damon said there were nine in all? Eleven? Caroline sipped at her port wine and tried to focus on Maresa's story about her family's summer relocation to Manhattan. The woman had led an interesting, though difficult life, and had met Cameron while working as a concierge for one of the family's resorts in St. Thomas. Her mother had multiple sclerosis, and her brother had suffered a traumatic brain injury after a car crash during one of their mother's seizures.

Apparently, both had found excellent health services and opportunities in New York City.

"My brother loves it here. He does landscaping work in a supervised program and is truly thriving." Maresa shifted on the sofa to face Caroline more fully, her amber-colored eyes striking against her darker skin tone. With her dark curls that ended in golden tips, she looked sun-kissed, even in the gray New York wintertime. "But enough about me. I insisted Cam bring me with him tonight so I could meet you. How are you feeling?"

"Fine." Caroline wasn't sure if anyone in this family knew about her ordeal being held against her will, or if the other woman was just curious about how her recovery from childbirth was going. "Damon took me sledding today in the park and it felt nice to be outdoors."

Maresa bit her lip. "Gabe said you had amnesia. Are you recovering any memories?"

"I may have remembered all that I can, but that doesn't mean I'm going to stop trying and hoping for more." She wasn't certain how much to share of her convoluted relationship with her father and the kidnapping she only recalled in pieces because of the drugs. "I'm seeing a new therapist tomorrow though, so maybe I'll learn some new strategies for digging through the hazy parts of my past."

"Good." Maresa reached over to lay a comforting hand on her arm. Her fingernails were painted a soft shade of lilac and a pear-shaped diamond surrounded by a halo of smaller diamonds glinted in the lamplight. "The important thing to know is that you're safe now and your husband loves you. I never saw a man so devastated as Damon when I met him last month—before you returned."

"Really?" she blurted before realizing that might come across as strange. But Maresa's words startled her, while also making her heart race. "I mean, I'm sure it was hard for him, but—"

Maresa leaned closer to lower her voice while Cameron and Damon looked over from across the room. "Honestly? I thought Damon looked haunted the first time I met him. He bears a resemblance to my husband, but there was a complete void in his eyes so different from how he looks now." She grinned and straightened, her gaze seeking the two men for a moment. "It's obvious he's found his happiness again. I'm so glad for you both."

Caroline's heart squeezed around the words, and the idea of her husband being that hurt by her disappearance. Could Maresa have read him correctly? Caroline was unsettled by how desperately she wanted to believe Damon's feelings ran that deep. Still…she didn't know this woman well enough to show her insecurity about her husband's affections.

"I forgot he came here then—right after he returned from his trip to Europe." She knew that he'd been searching for her.

So even if Damon didn't profess his love to her now,

didn't his actions during that horrible time prove that he loved her? Maybe she needed to dig deeper. To try harder to connect with him.

She'd just been so damn rattled by the way they'd laid silently together after making love.

Or what she'd thought had been making love.

With no promises of forever in her ear, no gentle words sweetly spoken, it didn't feel the same as before.

"Cameron likes him," Maresa confided. "And between you and me, I don't think he was prepared to like any of his half brothers. But he came here tonight with Malcom's power of attorney for the duration of the Transparent board meeting. They're prepared to help Damon however they can."

Caroline tensed at the mention of the meeting that was certain to be an ugly showdown between her dad and her husband. Two men she had once loved dearly. Now? She didn't understand her father, and she feared that Damon no longer returned her love. Whatever Maresa thought she'd seen in him—a new happiness— wasn't there as far as Caroline could tell.

"Malcolm won't be there when the board convenes?" She understood that Cameron would have his grandfather's authority, but she wondered if it would be as effective as having Malcolm McNeill there himself, an internationally recognized face of corporate success.

"You haven't heard?" Maresa peered toward the men again before returning her attention to Caroline. "I'm sure Damon will tell you after we leave either way. But

Malcolm is in Wyoming trying to make peace with the son who disowned him long ago."

"Liam?" She had no idea there was a rift between Damon's father and grandfather.

"No." Maresa shook her head and took a small sip of her port. "The *other* son that he never speaks about. Donovan."

Maresa filled her in on a few more details, but Caroline's brain was stuck wondering if Damon had known about this hidden branch of the family. Had he withheld the news from her?

It was one thing to make excuses for his reticence concerning his love for her after the way this year had torn them apart. But would he purposely shut her out of his private life now?

Then again, perhaps he didn't know about Malcolm's other son, either. There was a chance he was only just learning about it from Cameron, the way she'd just learned from Maresa. Perhaps they'd speak about it tonight and her fears that they would never heal the rift between them would be for nothing. She was simply rattled and unsettled because she was beginning to think she'd lost her chance at love.

Doing her best to dial back into the conversation, Caroline learned that Malcolm's ill health had made him decide to give the relationship with his estranged son one last try. Maresa assured her that Quinn, Cameron and Ian had all known about their uncle, but not one of them had ever met him since he'd been cut out of Malcolm's life when their father was just a teen.

There were McNeills all over Wyoming, successful ranchers who led a much different lifestyle than the real estate moguls, their East Coast relatives. Even the business news media failed to recall Malcolm's elder son when they wrote about him, a fact that explained why Caroline had never heard about those relations before.

As the evening came to a close and the men shook hands, Caroline thanked and hugged Maresa, a woman she would gladly view as a friend and ally down the road. Assuming, of course, Caroline remained a McNeill. Her gaze sought her husband's while they said their good-nights, wishing she could discern some small hint of the love Maresa had mentioned seeing in Damon.

When the door to the library closed behind Cameron and Maresa, who insisted they'd find their own way out, Caroline couldn't deny the pleasant shiver she felt as her husband wrapped two arms around her from behind and drew her back against his chest.

"You look so beautiful." His breath warmed her ear when he spoke. "I haven't been able to take my eyes off you all night."

Awareness stirred. Her pulse quickened at the feel of his whisker-roughened jaw against her neck as he bent to kiss her there. And yes, maybe she was far too willing to let go of the fears that had plagued her all evening. She needed this chance to be with him. To search for some hint of the love she wanted to feel in her marriage again.

"You appeared to be deep in conversation with your brother," she accused lightly, a secret thrill racing through her that he'd noticed the extra care she'd taken with her appearance.

"Not from the moment you set foot in the room." His hands skimmed her sides, lingering on her waist. "All I could think about was how soon I could get you out of this dress."

The fitted black dress was deceptively modest with a Nehru neckline that kept the bodice well covered. It was sleeveless, however, with a sexy cutout along one shoulder so that from the back it was decidedly racier. The asymmetrical crepe hem was knee-length on one side and thigh-grazing on the other. Silver snaps up one side gave it a rock n' roll edge.

And yes, she'd worn it with Damon in mind. They'd purchased it together from a design house in Italy on their honeymoon, and he'd liked it then, too. She'd brought it to New York with her, hoping it would bring them some of the romance and happiness of that time. Sure enough, the garment had worked some of its magic already.

"I seemed to recall you liked the snaps when we picked it out." She gripped his hand and steered it south along one hip where the silver snaps began.

His fingers brushed her bare thigh where the fabric ended, and she could feel his appreciation for the outfit pressing against her. She rolled her hips against him, only too glad to let the heat of this moment burn away everything else. She didn't know how much time she had left with Damon. She would damned well store up every moment of pleasure she could.

"I want you. Now." He flicked open a snap and she felt the cool rush of air against her thighs where the fabric slid open, almost to her panties.

"What if someone comes in?" She didn't know if the staff would be cleaning soon.

Then again, the feel of Damon's strong hand palming the front of her leg made her knees too weak to walk anywhere. Desire rushed through her. Hard.

"There's a private card room in back." He spun her around, taking her hand to close the distance to an entrance she hadn't noticed before, an opening disguised by one of the decorative lacquer panels. "This door locks."

They entered and he flipped on a light switch that illuminated a wine rack in the back of a circular red room with a long, mahogany bar. At the center sat a leather-topped poker table with five club chairs. The sound of a bolt sliding into place sent a ribbon of anticipation tickling its way up her spine.

Turning to face Damon, she watched his blue eyes darken to midnight. There was a naked hunger in his gaze that, for a moment, she swore had to be more than just physical need. It had to be.

They both craved this with a passion that went beyond sex.

Then, his hands were on her again and her brain switched off. He wrenched open the rest of the snaps on the dress in one easy swipe, baring her body. She'd worn red silk panties but no bra, her B-cups supported enough by the dress.

And now they were well supported by her husband's hands. His fingers roamed her curves, smoothing around the nipples and then gently plucking them, kissing each one in turn. A moan simmered from her and she pressed herself to him, arching up on her toes to position the V of her thighs closer to the hard heat of the ridge in his trousers.

His answering growl gave her another private thrill, stroking her feminine ego along with the fire inside. She wrapped her arms around his neck, desperate to be even closer. He lifted her up against him, steering her hips where she wanted them most, snug to his arousal.

He only left her there for a moment though, until he deposited her onto the heavy poker table, laying her on her back so her legs dangled off one side. The cool leather felt good against her back while she admired the view. He wrenched off his shirt, revealing the sculpted muscles she loved to touch. Then his hands moved lower, working fast but carefully as he unbuckled the belt and undid the buttons that kept him from her. She thought to repay him in kind, slipping a hand into her panties to give him access, but he halted her with an iron grip that gentled almost instantly.

"I'd like to." He whispered the word against her stomach before he dragged the silk down a few inches with his teeth.

More shivers danced over her. She tossed her head from one side to the other, ready for release, her hair tangling beneath her for a moment before he cupped her sex and touched her.

There.

The spasms were fast and hard, the orgasm a shock of sudden pleasure she hadn't been ready for. Her nails scratched against the table and he helped her ride the waves. When she had almost caught her breath, he entered her.

Fully.

Lost and clinging to him, she said his name like a mantra. Wrapping her arms around him, she could only hold on, the pleasure so intense. She kissed his face, savored the stubble-rough jaw and finally locked her ankles around him to hold him deep inside her.

He moved faster. Slower. He unwound her arms long enough to kiss her breasts again. When he took her mouth, he kissed her with devastating softness. Sweetness. Thoroughness.

All the while, he built a steady rhythm inside her that stole her breath.

When the second orgasm shook her, she saw stars behind her eyes. She hugged him tighter, feeling his release in the tensing of every muscle. Sensation drenched her, tugging her deeper into love.

So much so, she realized as consciousness slowly returned, that the mantra she'd been repeating against his skin all that time wasn't just idle sweet words.

It was: *I love you. I love you.*

The echo of the sentiment still hung in the small room, as if the words circled above their heads now that she'd said them aloud. Maybe hearing what Maresa had said, that Damon loved her, had given her the courage to say it tonight.

To hope he would say it back.

A year ago, it would have been perfectly normal for her to expect to hear it in return. But now, the room remained unnaturally silent except for their breathing.

Had she really said that?

Wrenching open her eyes, she peered up at him in the dimness only to see his gaze dart away as fast as hers alighted on him.

Her heart deflated along with all the hope she'd been feeling. Damon didn't love her. He was only with her to hold his family together.

They didn't speak about it as they dressed in silence, even though Damon tenderly kissed her temple and retrieved her clothes for her, even though he kept an arm around her as they walked to the elevator and rode it upstairs to their bedroom suites.

She would stay with him through the board meeting. Make sure she did everything in her power to help him win Transparent away from her father. But after that, she would have to walk away from this man who didn't trust her enough to love her anymore.

# Twelve

Three days later, Damon understood in no uncertain terms that he'd screwed up irrevocably. As in, there was no going back. He'd wrecked things with Caroline beyond repair. His chest ached with the knowledge as he watched her from the railing of the second-story patio of the house in Los Altos Hills. They'd flown back from Manhattan the day before to be in Silicon Valley for the Transparent board meeting today. Now, she jogged toward him as dawn broke to the east, her golden hair catching the slanting sunlight while Wade, the body-guard, kept tabs on her from a mountain bike.

She'd told Damon over dinner last night that she was working on her endurance so she could start pushing Lucas in a baby stroller while she jogged. And that had been about as much conversation as they'd shared since his colossal misstep with her that night in New York in the card room.

*I love you*, she'd told him.

And what did he say in response?

Nada. Zero. Zip.

He'd frozen up like a kid with his first girlfriend instead of a man intent on winning back his wife. He'd felt himself lock down at the notion of putting his heart in the line of fire again after the way she'd withheld Lucas from him when she returned. She'd believed the worst of him, thinking he didn't care that she'd disappeared.

"Dude?" His brother Gabe called to him from a seat at the patio table where he was shoveling down his second plate of eggs. He'd flown in from Martinique with his nine-month-old son so he could attend the board meeting. Jager was in the air now, scheduled to arrive before the ten o'clock start time. "Have you heard a word I've said over there?"

Damon forced himself to drag his gaze away from his wife. If he hadn't thought of a way to fix his mistake by now, chances were good he never would. There were some moments in life when a man didn't get a second chance, and he would have to live with that. Too bad the realization crushed the air out of his lungs until he could hardly draw a breath. Why hadn't he been able to simply return the words that might have kept her by his side forever?

He must still love her deeply or he wouldn't have

felt like he was free-falling into an abyss these past two days. The problem was, when she'd said those sweet words he wanted more than anything, he hadn't been certain they were true. How could she know how she felt when she didn't even remember their whole past? When she wasn't 100 percent certain if she'd walked out on him or if she'd truly been forcefully taken from their home?

She'd turned to her father when she was pregnant with his child. Hadn't she felt any of that love for Damon then? He stalked back toward the table where Gabe sat with his son Jason squirming on his lap. The kid was already a handful, crawling all over the place, climbing anything and everything, with a willful disposition tempered by the cutest grin imaginable.

"Honestly?" Damon tried and failed to remember a single thing his brother had been saying to him as he gladly plucked baby Jason off Gabe's lap so the guy could finish his eggs in peace. "I'm more than a little distracted today."

He set his wiggly nephew down on the rug in the middle of the patio deck so the kid had some room to scoot. Would Lucas look like this in another seven months? He didn't want to miss another day of his son's life, yet if he didn't fix things with Caroline...

He couldn't even fathom the future.

"Yeah. No kidding. And I'm trying to adjust to the time change when I've barely slept for days after the latest nanny quit, but I'm still making an effort to converse like a normal human being." Draining the last swig of orange juice in his glass, Gabe scraped his chair back from the wrought iron table. "I've been trying to tell you that you're an idiot to delay talking to her."

"And tell her what?" Damon sidestepped Jason's path as he crawled like his diaper was on fire toward some red blocks that Gabe had brought out of the nursery with him. "The truth? That I didn't trust her enough to believe she loved me?" He shook his head. "That's only going to make her pack her bags faster."

He'd tried to speak to Caroline's therapist back in Vancouver, to solicit the woman's advice for talking to her, but the doctor had held firm that she wouldn't discuss any issues that could compromise Caroline's privacy.

"No." Gabe rose from his chair, his white button-down and tan cargo shorts about as formal as the guy ever dressed outside of a meeting like the one they'd have to attend today. His work at the Birdsong Hotel definitely ran to the informal. But there was nothing casual or relaxed about his expression now as he stalked toward Damon. "First thing you do is let her know you love her. Fix that screw-up before anything else, because I guarantee you, that's killing her."

Gabe stood shoulder-to-shoulder with him, watching over Jason as the baby tried to eat one of the fat red blocks. Damon was grateful for the distraction from the topic since the accusation his brother had just leveled had found its mark.

"I think she's angry more than anything." He knew because she'd hardly spoken to him. But she was harder to read now than before her disappearance. His wife was quieter. In the past, if she was upset with him, she would have told him why in no uncertain terms.

And since that night in New York, he'd buried himself in work, preparing for his appointment with the Transparent investors. With a wince of guilt, he realized how quickly he'd fallen into that old pattern. Back when she'd gone to London to make amends with her father, he'd been upset and had retreated to his office on the West Coast. He had regretted not talking to her more rationally then, yet now he followed the same path. Avoidance.

"Is that how you'd feel if someone you loved left you hanging when you put your heart on the line? Angry?" Gabe shook his head. "I'm not saying I have the best instincts where women are concerned, though. Maybe I was never lucky enough to find a really good one." He scooped Jason off the floor, lifting the baby high over his head long enough to make the kid smile. Then he swooped him down low, while the boy squealed happily. "All I know is you don't just sit back and watch while a woman like Caroline walks away."

His brother started to leave, shaking Damon out of his thoughts.

"Gabe." He appreciated his younger sibling's insights, especially now when Jager was so happy with his own wife that Damon would never ask him about this. "What if she eventually remembers what happened that day she disappeared? What if she wakes up one day and recalls that she left me because she wanted it to be over?" He had played the scenarios over and over in his head, grappling with those fears that he wasn't a good husband. But how would he ever be a better one if he didn't change? "Maybe she didn't run into trouble with the guys who abducted her until she had set up a life apart from me."

Gabe stalked back toward him, his expression stark. In contrast, Jason kicked and drooled, gumming one finger while he grinned.

"Wake up, brother." Gabe spoke the words just inches from Damon's face before he leaned back. "None of that matters. Or if it does, count yourself lucky you got another chance with someone who loves you *right now*. Today. That's a whole lot more than most people get."

There was a wealth of feeling behind the words, making Damon wonder what kinds of hell his brother had dealt with that he knew nothing about.

That was a conversation for another day, though. Right now, Damon needed to head into the office for the professional battle of his life. With any luck, the police would be there afterward to ask his father-in-law all the questions about their investigation he'd avoided while he was overseas.

It was probably too much to hope that Stephan Degraff would be dragged off to jail then and there for giving false statements to the police. But if it came to seeing Stephan behind bars or keeping Caroline, Damon knew what he would choose.

Because his brother was right. Damon might not deserve a second chance with her, but since he'd been fortunate enough to get one, he needed to try and convince her they were worth it.

He just hoped it wasn't too late.

Caroline paced outside the penthouse boardroom of the Transparent building later that morning, trying to time her entrance to the most important business meeting of her husband's life.

Her husband. For now.

She stopped short, her gaze moving from the stunning view of the Santa Cruz Mountains outside the reception area windows down to the wedding band set on her fingers. Pausing at one of the floor-to-ceiling windows, Caroline indulged herself for a moment, staring at the diamond, tilting it this way and that to catch the best light and refract it so that little rainbow squares danced across the polished bamboo floors.

Damon needed her help today, even if he didn't know it. He'd allowed her to ride into the office with him and his brother, Gabe, although he'd insisted she wait outside the meeting with her bodyguards. They'd brought two, knowing that her father would be in attendance. But Damon had asked her not to sit in on the contentious conference, even though her former job title would have given her every right to do so.

She understood that he might see her as a distraction today when he needed to be on top of his game to out-maneuver her father. What Damon didn't understand was that he had no chance of beating Stephan Degraff without her help. Her father was hellbent on revenge. She saw that now. Stephan would do anything to thwart Damon if only for the sake of proving to her that Damon wasn't worth her time.

Her love.

Her father was wrong about that. Damon was the worthiest man in the world for that honor. If only he loved her back.

Yet to help make things right for her husband, she would have to be the one to maneuver her father. She could convince him to sign that paper and give Damon the ultimate win. But Damon wasn't going to like it one bit.

Not that it should matter now. He'd already broken her heart with his profound silence following her dec-laration of love. Except, foolishly perhaps, she didn't want to hurt him any more than she already had. Keep-ing his child a secret from him had been more than he should have to bear.

Behind her, the elevator chimed. Her bodyguards didn't move, and yet she could feel their readiness for anything.

"Mrs. McNeill?" A familiar police officer stepped off the elevator onto the top floor, his dark jacket and plain blue tie setting him apart from most of the staffers at Transparent. From the coders to the front office workers, the company embraced a more relaxed, West Coast vibe.

"Officer Downey." She strode forward to shake his hand. "My husband made sure I wasn't in the building when my father entered, but he's in the boardroom now." She pointed to the meeting space where Damon had been joined by his brothers Jager and Gabe, plus his half brother, Cameron.

Beyond the McNeill men, there were five other attendees, including her dad. An administrative assistant sat off to one side, taking notes. They could see the proceedings through the clear glass wall on one side that gave the meeting room a mountain view, but still allowed the light to spill into the interior reception area.

Fortunately, her father's back was to her.

She needed to steel herself to face the man who had ruined her marriage and tried to keep Damon from his child.

"We've spoken at length with the man who asked for your husband at the Los Altos Hills house a few days back," the officer informed her, peeling off his aviator shades and tucking them in his pocket. "We have some good leads on two of the suspects we believe served as your captors in Mexico. Once we speak to your father, we'll know more. But I will warn you, it appears your father has business ties to both of them, as well."

She wanted to ask him if he thought her dad could have really masterminded the kidnapping of his own daughter, but she knew he wouldn't answer such a thing. How could anyone have suspected that? She'd known her father was controlling, but she'd never guessed he would try to erase her memory to keep her away from Damon. Whatever her father did, if she couldn't prove it and see him punished, she would have to find a way to live with it. To move past it.

"Thank you." She nodded, needing to keep her thoughts on the task in front of her and not her spiraling emotions. If she wanted her father to sign over his stake in Transparent, she needed to put on a hell of a show in that boardroom. "If you'll excuse me though, I think I see my cue to enter the meeting starting right now."

She watched as Damon shoved a contract in front of her father. He was passing over the buyout offer with incentives to sell his stake to the McNeills. There were terms Stephan Degraff would never agree to.

Unless she made him.

"Are you sure?" Officer Downey stepped forward, as if he would follow her into the meeting. "I can go with you."

"I'll be fine." She tried for a gracious smile, all the while knowing how important timing was for the entrance. "I have two bodyguards and you can see me through the window."

Her heart beat faster in fear of her father, of what she might discover. Damon would be angry about this. But the end would justify the means.

She hoped. It was the best way she could think of

to make amends for not finding her way back to him sooner. She peeled off her wedding ring set and slid the diamonds into her purse.

She couldn't afford to think about those vows right now when she was about to break them in spectacular fashion.

"I would have to agree to the sale, and I never will." Stephan Degraff had the nerve to smile as he refused to even glance at the agreement in front of him. It was a small, fake-apologetic smile that Damon wanted to punch into next year.

He wouldn't, of course.

He wasn't going to lose his cool in the boardroom, especially now when the stakes were higher than they'd ever been before. The safety of his wife and his child rested in the balance.

It was just because of the hell this pale, perfectly groomed man had put Caroline through that had Damon imagining all the ways to exact revenge. How dare the bastard show his face after lying to the police about Caroline's disappearance. The guy had always been somewhat of a Silicon Valley enigma, focusing on start-ups that other investors hadn't even heard about before, beating his competition to the punch. Damon suspected that had far more to do with his daughter's business savvy than his own. The value of Degraff's portfolio had skyrocketed once Caroline had joined his company.

And the bastard had paid her back by sabotaging her marriage. Her health.

Risking the life of his own grandson in the process.

The knowledge made Damon tense with icy rage, but he had to get through this. Had to turn the tide before the man succeeded in robbing him of his company.

Everything about Stephan Degraff was meticulous, from his perfectly centered double Windsor knot to the way he put down his pen at a ninety-degree angle to the top of his legal pad every time. He was a perfectionist who took things too damned far.

"Has it occurred to you that it's generous of the company to offer a buyout now when you might be sitting in prison this time next week, without any way to tap into the rewards of your investment at all?" Damon ground his teeth while Gabe kicked his shin.

Little did Gabe know how much he'd restrained himself already.

"Prison?" The bastard lifted an eyebrow, his lips pursing in a smirk. "I hardly think so."

"The terms are generous," Cameron McNeill stepped in smoothly, redirecting the conversation away from prison time and giving Damon a moment to get his fury under control. "And this way you're not tied to the launch of the new product for a payout. You must realize we can continue to stall the launch if we can't agree on terms."

There was grumbling around the dark cypress wood table from the other investors, none of whom wanted to wait another day for their investment to appreciate, let alone months.

Damon didn't care. He needed control of his business. And now, even if Degraff agreed to stop trying to boot him out of the CEO seat, it was no longer enough. Damon needed the backstabbing prick gone.

He lifted his eyes toward the glass wall separating the meeting space from the reception area, and glimpsed Caroline talking to the cop who was working on the investigation into her disappearance. Damn it. What was she doing in such a visible spot? He'd hoped she would wait in one of the offices. What if her father saw her?

The need to run out of the meeting and take her somewhere safe was making it impossible to concentrate.

"I know that you're trying to remove me." Stephan Degraff flipped his black Montblanc fountain pen in the other direction, oblivious to his daughter standing so close to him on the other side of the glass. That damn pen remained perfectly perpendicular to the edge of his pad, but was now facing the other way. "I understand that you don't want me to have a role in Transparent. But you've taken my daughter. You won't take my stake in the business."

Damon hadn't even processed that remark when the conference room door swished open. The click of her high heels had an authoritative sound as Caroline entered and made her way across the room.

Stunning every single person in the room.

Her hair was brushed to shining silk, a shade lighter than it had been just the day before. He hadn't noticed that in the car on the drive over; he was too distracted thinking about the meeting. In fact, even her clothes were different from the things she'd worn earlier in the week. This was Caroline Degraff, executive in charge. Her stiletto pumps made her tower over the table. Her white fitted dress had been tailored to the leaner frame of her body.

"Don't be ridiculous." She kept her eyes on her father as she entered the room. "Damon hasn't taken me, Dad." She smiled warmly at him. The dutiful, perfect daughter, reunited with her lying bastard of a father.

Betrayal stabbed Damon.

*Dad?* That's how she thought of the scum who had lied through his teeth about her disappearance? This was the same man responsible for keeping Damon from his son. Had she been lying to Damon all week? He could not imagine how she could still be loyal to this miserable excuse for a human being.

His brain couldn't comprehend it. He watched her drop into the empty chair beside Stephan Degraff, who almost looked like he'd seen a ghost. Had he not expected to see Caroline? Or was he expecting to see a different version of his daughter, the weak and confused amnesiac he'd tried to manipulate for his own ends?

For once, Damon could identify with her smarmy father. He didn't know what to believe, either, but he sure as hell understood what it meant that she no longer wore her wedding ring. She'd made sure the whole room would know where her real allegiance lay.

Bile burned his gut.

"Caroline." Stephan Degraff gripped his pen harder, clearly trying to compose himself. "You're here."

"Of course." She smiled that high-wattage grin that Damon remembered from the honeymoon photos. "Where else would I be? I'm all about protecting the family interests." She passed him her pen, a Montblanc that matched her father's except it was silver. "I've had the benefit of reading the agreement ahead of time, and the terms are very generous, especially considering how we know about the glitch in the launch product."

There were more murmurs around the table. Was she talking about the security issue Damon's hacker had found? The one she knew Damon had already patched?

He straightened in his seat, trying to follow whatever she was doing. Damon might not comprehend her motive, but one thing was certain. Having her father sign that paper benefited Damon.

Not Stephan.

And Caroline knew it better than anyone.

"McNeill, is that true?" a worried voice asked loudly over the fray. "Is the launch product flawed?"

That seemed to be the concern around the table for anyone who wasn't a McNeill or a Degraff. They didn't want to think their investment had gone belly-up because of a glitch.

Thankfully, Gabe responded for him while Damon watched the drama play out between Caroline and her father on the opposite side of the table. Stephan Degraff stared at her in wonder, like he'd recovered the most precious thing in the world to him.

To a certain extent, Damon could empathize. He hadn't wanted to lose her, either. But he sure as hell wouldn't kidnap or drug someone he cared about to force them into staying loyal to him. That wasn't love. That was obsession.

"You really think I should sign, Caroline?" Stephan Degraff took the pen she'd given him, his hand poised over the contract.

For the first time since he'd entered the room, the bastard appeared confused. Conflicted. Something in his tone of voice revealed how much he wanted his daughter to be on side.

Damon held his breath.

He wanted Caroline on *his* side, too. And in that moment, he realized how much more important it was to win her than Transparent. He'd been battling so hard to keep his company when all along what he should have been fighting for was the woman herself.

Caroline slid the papers out from under her father's elbow, flipping to a back page. "I do. This is very fair to the Degraff interests. We need to protect our investment and get out before Transparent tanks." She slid the contract back under his pen and leaned closer to touch the bastard's arm. "I know how important our family is to you."

It was all Damon could do not to launch over the table and tear her away from Stephan. But one thing was becoming clear. She wasn't betraying Damon at all, no matter how it appeared. The deal wasn't going to help the Degraff interests one bit.

She was playing her father for all he was worth to make sure he signed the paper that gave Damon control of Transparent.

"There is nothing more important." Sweat beads popped along the man's pale forehead as he swore the words like an oath. "I would do anything to keep our family safe, Caroline. I'm glad you know that."

A smile stretched the bastard's thin lips as he stared up at the daughter he must care about in some twisted way.

Then Damon watched his primary investor scratch his name in ink on the contract and tossed down the pen like a gauntlet.

Damon almost couldn't believe his eyes. He heard someone—his brothers, maybe—trading discreet high-fives. Then Jager clearly told one of the other investors there was no problem with the launch and that it was as hack-proof as possible.

Cameron rose from the table and went around to shake Stephan's hand. "Since you've sold your shares to me, Mr. Degraff, I'll have my attorney escort you out so he can sign the funds over while the rest of the investors finish up the meeting."

"Of course." Stephan nodded, though he watched the byplay around the table uncertainly, as if becoming aware he may have missed something. "I look forward to being done with the McNeills." He held out an arm for his daughter. "Caroline?"

Damon held his breath. He couldn't allow her to walk out of this room with that man. Their marriage may have fallen apart, but he would never let anything happen to her on his watch.

"I need to stay a bit longer, Dad," she told him gently. "Just to hammer out a few details about my own stake in the company." She opened the file folder that had been in front of the empty seat at the table, which contained a projected timetable for the new product launch. "I'll be along shortly."

With her perfect posture and thoughtful scrutiny of the pages in front of her, she gave every appearance of being all business. But Damon saw the way the blue vein in her neck ticked like mad, the pulse tapping triple time.

He was an idiot. And he wasn't worthy of the woman who'd just handed him the biggest business victory of his life after he'd hurt her. He wanted to roar with fury at himself as the rest of the room cheered Degraff's departure. Everyone but Caroline, of course, who turned sad eyes to watch Officer Downey escort her protesting father into another room.

Thanks to her, Damon had regained control of Transparent. But he couldn't imagine a more hollow victory when he'd lost her in the process.

"Congratulations, brother." Cameron McNeill hauled Damon to his feet and pulled him in for a bear hug. "We're going to make beautiful business together, mate."

Damon nodded. Thanked him. But when Gabe thumped him on the back and pointed to the conference room door closing, Damon realized his wife had made a quiet exit.

Shit.

He scrambled toward the door.

"Excuse me." He clapped a hand on Jager's shoulder, the brother who'd taken the reins at this company plenty of times in the past. "Jager will finish the meeting. I have to go."

# Thirteen

A uniformed officer and a female detective Caroline hadn't met before whisked her father away before she even arrived in the reception area. She met her father's cold, furious gaze as he backed stiffly into the elevator cabin, flanked by his two escorts.

Lifting her chin, she allowed herself to meet his eyes without flinching. To let him know she'd recovered—if not her memory, damn it, her dignity. Her self-respect.

It was a small consolation considering everything else she'd lost this week. A love that she'd once thought was strong enough to overcome anything. Her husband.

Her chest had ached more each day following the cold ending to their encounter in the card room. Now, the hurt and hollowness inside would have brought her to her knees if not for Lucas. She still had a precious son to mother and her love for her child would have to keep her strong.

"Caroline." The deep rumble of Damon's voice sounded behind her in the reception area.

She turned around to find him closing in on her, his steps muffled by the Aztec-patterned rug in the lobby. She glanced into the meeting room where Damon's older brother Jager seemed to be leading the meeting, all eyes turned toward him.

"Shouldn't you be in there?" She wondered what he thought of her performance in the conference room. Was he going to rebuke her for pointing out the flaw in the software to the conference room at large? She wanted to believe he'd seen through her guise of camaraderie with Stephan, but then again, Damon didn't trust her much anymore. Maybe he would see that calculated risk she'd taken as yet another betrayal. "Your meeting is still going."

He joined her near the windows overlooking the Santa Cruz Mountains, in the corner farthest from the small reception desk where an administrator sat with a Bluetooth in one ear as she tapped her computer keys.

"I've waited too long to talk to you already. Jager can finish up in there without me."

"Your investors need your guidance. Your reassurance." She understood all too well about how fickle investors could be. Her father got antsy at the slightest hint of unease in a company that he'd backed. "I thought it was worth leaking the information about the software glitch to convince my father I had his best interests at heart."

"You've given the remaining investors the best possible reassurance already by relieving the board of the one consistently dissenting opinion." His blue eyes searched hers. "I wish you'd been there to receive the thanks we all owe you for making that deal happen."

She felt a spike of relief that he'd recognized what she had been angling to accomplish. They still understood each other at some level, at least.

"You knew what I was doing then?" She flicked a thumb over the empty place on her ring finger, remembering how bare that spot felt.

"I'm not going to pretend I didn't have a moment of…" He seemed to search for the right words. Behind them, the phone rang, and his brow furrowed. "Look, Caroline, I really need to talk to you, but not here. Could we go to my office?"

Her mind traveled back a year to late nights working on plans for the company when they would lock his office door and take a break from the job in the most rewarding way possible. She wasn't sure she could sit in those chairs where they'd made love.

Not now.

"How about we speak in my office instead?" Maybe it was the business victory with her father making her feel newly emboldened. She guessed that when the adrenaline let-down kicked in, she was going to have to start dealing with the hurt and regret of discovering her father had gone to criminal lengths to separate her from Damon. But she couldn't think about that right now if she was going to negotiate a future apart from Damon.

She needed to work from a position of strength before her heart broke the rest of the way.

"No problem." Damon nodded. "You still have a key? I'm sure the cleaning staff have maintained it, but I haven't been in there since the day I let the police go through your things."

His words helped her to recall how much he'd been through, as well. This year had been so painful for them both. She reached in her bag and withdrew her key ring before leading the way down the hall.

Despite her outward bravado, her hands were a little unsteady as she worked the lock and opened the door. She turned on the lights to the penthouse corner office, a spread that equaled his in amenities.

Only now, of course, the administrator's seat out front was vacant. Caroline hadn't worked a day at Transparent since she'd departed for her honeymoon, but the space was precisely as she remembered. Unlike the rest of Transparent's hypermodern offices, she'd chosen to complement the views from the floor-to-ceiling windows with bookshelves on every other wall. White linen swags draped along the tops of the shelves and the windows. Her cream leather office chair sat behind an antique desk, which was painted another shade of eggshell and hand-rubbed for a distressed effect. Birch branches stood in a wooden pitcher in place of flowers on one corner of the desk.

Here, the books, the framed photos, and the stunning mountain views provided all the color. A framed photo of Damon and her sat prominently on one bookshelf. The two of them seated together on a park bench in the gardens of the Winchester Mystery House. She wore a blue dress with white polka dots, a fanciful, romantic sundress with a fuller skirt than she normally chose. Wide-set straps showed off the necklace she'd bought in the gift shop that day, a glass daisy inspired by one of the windows in the home.

Seeing that necklace—a piece she hadn't seen in months—brought back a flood of new memories. The streak of thoughts through her head came so fast it almost hurt. She reeled back a little from the photo, the day of her kidnapping returning to her mind.

"Caroline?" Damon was beside her, his hand on her waist. Then, he shifted it to her shoulder when she still wobbled. "Are you all right?"

"My father was there." She blurted the worst of it, needing to share the burden of those painful moments. "My God. He was in our house that day they took me."

"Sit down." He guided her into a spot on the love seat near the windows, the stiff white denim fabric yielding under their weight as they sat down together. "You remembered something?"

Just two days ago she'd sat across the room from a therapist in New York who'd told her she might never recover her memories. But now, new information flooded her neuropathways, making connections throughout her brain in a way that felt like her whole head was lighting up.

"The necklace I'm wearing in that photo." She pointed to the picture of them on the park bench. "I was wearing it on the flight back from London."

Damon left her side for a moment to retrieve the image for a closer look. Lowering himself back to the loveseat, he set the silver picture frame on the low table near a stack of books on gardening.

"I bought you the replica of one of the daisy windows you liked." His full attention returned to her, his hand smoothing light, comforting circles between her shoulder blades. "It was just a fun, lunchtime trip to get out of the office. I put daisies in your hair that day, too."

Her heart hugged the memory close. How could she lose this man now when she was only fully appreciating how much he'd meant to her?

"Right. It was a happy time and I liked wearing that daisy." She closed her eyes, remembering. "I heard someone in the house a couple of hours after I got back to the Los Altos Hills place. I hoped maybe it was you, coming home early to surprise me, because who else enters a house without knocking?" She shook her head, her chest tight. "I guess I'd left the door unlocked though, and the security system hadn't been hooked up yet."

"I was furious with the security company when I

realized there were no cameras going the day you disappeared." Damon nodded, his expression grave. He looked impossibly handsome in his navy suit and custom tailored shirt. "I fired them for not having everything up and running when you returned. Then I hired a whole new company to redo every bit of the job."

She thought back to Maresa's insistence that Damon had been a wreck without her. How could it be too late to recover their love if it had run so deep? She dragged in another steadying breath.

"When I went downstairs, my father was in our house. He'd flown here the day before me, hoping to convince me to leave you since he hadn't managed to do that when I saw him in London." Her fingers clenched into fists as the time washed over her, blooming in bright red bursts of pain. His cruelty had been shocking. Painful. "I was angry to see him, but I attempted to be civil even though he'd brought two goons with him I didn't know. I thought they were his private security. I didn't realize until later they were there for me."

She no longer needed the police to tell her the role her father had played in her disappearance. She remembered.

A gust of air from the ventilation system sent a chill through her and she shivered.

"I'm so sorry I wasn't there to protect you." Damon brushed his hand over her hair where it trailed down her back. "So damned sorry."

"I would have never guessed he would try something so…" She shook her head, then steadied herself by looking into Damon's eyes as he patiently let her find her way through wave after wave of emotions. "He went ballistic about the necklace." That had tipped her off to the heartbreaking—terrifying—realization that Stephan Degraff had moved from eccentric and controlling to full-on obsessive. "He said cheap trinkets were beneath me. He ripped it off my throat." Her hand went to her neck, remembering the scrape of his nails on her skin as he took it. "He wrestled off my wedding rings, too. I was screaming so much, one of his guards had to restrain me."

Damon hugged her closer, his lips brushing her temple. "The police have him. You'll never have to deal with him again, I promise you, on my life, I promise."

"I know." She breathed deep, trying to regain that sense of strength she'd felt after she tricked her father into signing away his share of Transparent, but she found herself needing Damon's support to sustain her through the past steamrolling over her. "I told him to leave, but he refused. He said he would have me committed for unstable behavior. Then those goons grabbed me and—" Things got a little hazier after that.

"It's okay," Damon soothed. "Take your time. You're safe. I have you."

She tried to slow down her breathing, needing to press through before the fog once again overtook the memories. "They gave me a drink in the limo, trying to make me calm down even though they'd tied my hands.

My father had already left in his own car while I went with the two muscle-heads. By then I was truly terrified. I took the drink and didn't scream because they said they could get one of my siblings next, but that's how they drugged me the first time."

"Your father must have stayed behind to leave your wedding bands and pack a few of your things." Not letting go of her, Damon pulled his phone from his pocket with his other hand. "I'm going to text Officer Downey that you have additional evidence so he knows to keep your father in custody."

It would be so easy to tip her head onto Damon's shoulder. To soak in every bit of comfort she could from his presence. But she knew walking away from him would be even more harder if she gave in to that impulse now.

"Thank you." She straightened, telling herself to keep it together. "I know you wanted to talk to me privately, and instead, I've dominated the conversation completely." Her heart ached for her husband and the love they used to share.

He set his phone aside. "What you remembered was too important to risk delaying. I couldn't be happier for your sake that your memory is coming back. I can't imagine how frustrating it's been for you missing pieces of the past."

He took her hand. Squeezed. She had to close her eyes to prevent herself from overthinking the simple gesture. She wanted it to mean so much more.

"Thank you for understanding," she said finally, her throat dry, her eyes burning with tears for her failed marriage. "But please, tell me. What did you want to talk about?"

Nodding, he shifted beside her. "I wanted to see you alone to ask you for another chance to prove to you that I love you and trust you. I—" He took a deep breath, his blue eyes darker with emotion. "I know that doesn't mean much for me to tell you now, after you've proven your loyalty beyond all doubt." He shook his head. "I should have told you before. I never stopped loving you, Caroline. Not even when it hurt the most."

It scared her how much she wanted to believe him. So she stuffed down all the hope that wanted to dance to life inside her to focus on what he was saying. She needed to be sure.

"Why should I believe you?" She felt tears sting the backs of her eyes that she would need to question him after he'd told her the words she'd longed to hear. "I have to ask, Damon, because you've had days to return the feelings I shared with you. And instead, you retreated into your work and pushed me out."

She couldn't be married to a man who didn't share her love. She had thought Damon was so different from her father. Open and warm. Ready to play and let work slide sometimes to simply enjoy life and be. The daisy necklace had reminded her of that. Of the simple pleasures.

*Like winter picnics in Central Park?* a contrary voice

inside her asked. Maybe she had seen signs of his play-ful side since her return. But she needed him to trust her, too.

Outside her office, she heard voices in the reception area. The meeting must have broken up. But Damon didn't move to join them.

"Things happened so fast between us when we fell in love." His knee brushed hers as he spoke, a warm stroke of wool-gabardine on her bare knee. "I probably should have questioned it more at that time, but it was the most exciting, passionate love I'd ever experienced, and I couldn't wait to just make you all mine."

"Me, too." Her throat burned at the thought of losing that. Still, he'd said that he loved her. "That's how I felt."

"But maybe we didn't take enough time to really think about how we could fit together long-term. When we argued after the honeymoon, it felt like the end of the world to me. That's the only reason I could believe for a second that you'd walked away on your terms and left me. I figured I hadn't lived up to my end of the fairy-tale relationship and I lost you." He stroked a strand of her hair that lay on the shoulder closest to him.

Her scalp tingled.

Maybe his love was still there after all?

"I couldn't wait to see you and make up with you when I got home." She knew that for certain. "But even if I was upset, I wouldn't just walk out. For better or worse, Damon, my father did raise me to be the kind of woman who works hard at everything. And I would never give up on something so easily."

"I should have known that. And when you came back…" He shook his head, the emotions and regret evident in his eyes. "I was ready to do anything to make you stay forever. To fix anything I'd messed up the first time. So when I realized you'd been keeping secrets—"

"For Lucas." She wanted to be clear about that. "I couldn't risk revealing him to you until I knew for sure what your feelings were toward me. My father has been feeding me a diet of lies for months, showing me stories about the McNeills and telling me you married me to inherit—"

"None of it was true." His jaw tensed, showing a streak of pride and stubbornness that she admired. Something about his expression made her imagine what Lucas would look like one day. Would he take after his father with that same McNeill pride?

Would she be with them both to see that day?

The hope she'd stuffed down before grew back stronger. More insistent.

"I know that now. But between the drugs and being ill and having amnesia, I questioned everything. Every. Single. Thing." She realized that no matter what the outcome of this conversation, she loved him as much— more—than ever.

"That's what a good mother would do." He stroked a hand along her arm. "I'm sorry, Caroline. I understand now that you had to make the call to put Lucas first while I was still concentrating on us—fixated on why you left. I'm trying to catch up to be a good father."

"And you are." She liked seeing him hold their son. Kiss the baby's silky hair. "I trust that. But what I really want to know is, what's next for us?"

Of all the risks she'd taken today—maneuvering her father into thinking she was on his side, gambling with Damon's company in front of his other investors—this one was the biggest. Because Damon McNeill still held her heart.

"If I had my way, we would go to the police station right now to tell them everything you've remembered. While you give your statement, I'd work on making arrangements to have legal custody of your brothers shifted over to you so that we can help them through this." His hand moved to her knee. "My father went missing from my life at their age, and I know how confusing that will be for them."

Tipping her head to Damon's shoulder, she couldn't wait another moment to take the comfort he offered. Not when he said the most beautiful things. She appreciated that he would think of her family—her father's sons—in that way.

"You're right. Thank you for considering my brothers' needs." She kissed his shoulder through his jacket. No matter what, Damon was going to be an amazing role model. And maybe, her heart hoped, he would be so much more.

"I think we should pull them out of school. Let them spend a few weeks with us here, or maybe in Martinique. That's a good place for kids." He frowned as he seemed to weigh two important choices. Then he lifted his head. "Maybe we ask them?"

"I think that's a great idea." She felt a smile from deep inside her, confidence gathering along with the hope. This feeling couldn't be wrong. She remembered it from those heady weeks when she'd fallen in love with this man. They clicked. They fit together.

Damon nodded. Then he took both her hands in his, turning to face her more fully on the sofa. "But first, I want to ask you to forgive me for not telling you how much I love you. Today, yesterday, and every day since I met you." He stroked the backs of her fingers. "I was tongue-tied and stupid that night you said it to me. My brain was stuck wondering how you could feel that way about me. But not for a moment of that time did I not love you back." His voice lowered, the emotions behind the words so evident she couldn't believe she hadn't heard them before. "Please believe me."

The rightness of the moment, the truth of their happiness, flowed over her. Comforting her. Assuring her. Making her heart whole again.

"I do." She kissed his cheek, let a tear of happiness roll unchecked down her face. "I believe you. Because whether you say it or not, I feel your love all around me right now. It's been there all along, I was just too afraid to believe it. It's in the thoughtful things you do for me and the way you took care of Victoria with the bodyguard. Or putting my brothers' care before anything else today."

"I would do anything for you. I knew it in that board meeting that I'd rather lose the company a hundred times over than lose you for even one more day." He kissed her fallen tear and both of her closed eyes. "Will you do one thing for me, my sweet Caroline?"

"What is it, my love?"

"Will you let me put your wedding rings on again?" He took up her left hand and kissed the bare third finger. "I keep putting them right here and they keep disappearing."

She laughed. "Yes." Digging in her purse, she couldn't help the relieved laughter that kept coming. Everything was going to work out for her and Damon and their family. "But you have to admit I had a good reason for taking them off this time."

"The best." Smiling, he took the two bands from her and slid them into place. "You slayed me back there when you walked into the meeting and took charge."

She flexed her fingers, admiring the sparkle of diamonds in the sunlight through the huge windows, the sense of rightness filling her.

"It will always hurt—what my father did to me." There would be a hole in her heart that nothing else would fill, but she looked forward to connecting with Damon's family. To finding more role models for her son, and to strengthening her own support network with friendships like she'd started with Maresa. "But it felt good to shut him out of Transparent forever."

"You are an incredible woman on every level, Mrs. McNeill." He leaned closer to kiss her neck. "I'm going to have the most stunning daisy necklace made for you to replace the old one."

Her skin heated where he kissed it. "I actually really liked the gift shop trinket." She skimmed a hand under his jaw to cup his face and looked in his blue eyes.

"You want another necklace from the gift shop?"

She thought about why the impromptu present had pleased her so much the first time.

"For my whole life, I was taught to be the best. That second wasn't good enough." She'd been trained from early childhood and she was ready to break free of the mold. "I don't want to strive for perfection anymore. I want to know that our love is strong enough it can bear a misstep and we'll trust in each other to get through it." She warmed to her theme, imagining a future by Damon's side. "I want to take spontaneous walks in the middle of the workday and not feel guilty about it. I want to play. To have fun. To just be."

"I can do all of that." He wrapped her up in his arms. "I can play and have fun, I swear. But I'm still going to work my tail off not to make any more mistakes with you."

"Just love me the way I love you." She felt confident saying it because she knew it would be returned in full. Maybe even with interest. "That's all I need."

"I'm so glad to have my wife back." He kissed her lips. Slowly. Thoroughly. "You can't imagine how happy that makes me."

Actually, she had a very good idea because it made her glow inside to be reunited with him. But for now, she simply closed her eyes so she could feel the love all around her.

# Epilogue

*One month later*

Damon bent over the portacrib and settled his son onto the sheet covered with smiling blue jellyfish. Two weeks ago, he'd relocated his whole family to a private bungalow at the Birdsong Hotel, the property his brother Gabe owned in Martinique. He'd felt the need to solidify the new, expanded family dynamic that included Lucas, Caroline and Caroline's two younger brothers. Even Victoria had requested a leave of absence from her university program to join them for a week. New McNeills and honorary McNeills filled two bungalows of the Birdsong, giving them time to play together on the shore of the Caribbean, safely away from the headlines about Stephan Degraff back home.

As Damon watched Lucas huff out a sleepy sigh, his arms flung wide in that careless, baby way, Damon's heart filled with love. Again. The way it did dozens of times a day as he marveled at how full his life had become in such a short time. He'd gone from a year of devastated loneliness to having a beautiful wife and three sons. One by blood, two by law.

He wouldn't be able to adopt the boys, as much as he would love to, since their father would never sign any more paperwork that would benefit Damon. But Caroline's brothers knew they would always have a real family now, and they were excited about the idea of attending public schools and being under the same roof as their sister and baby nephew.

Damon turned on the nursery monitor for Lucas's nap even though he wasn't venturing far from the crib. He didn't mind sitting on the deck of the bungalow with the baby monitor while he watched Caroline cavort on the beach with her siblings. Damon double-checked the video feed on the nursery monitor before he dimmed the lights so his boy could rest and dream of happy times.

Stepping out of the baby's room, Damon wandered out onto the patio to find his brother Gabe already there, sprawled on a deck lounger, a silver bucket full of ice and bottled beers at his feet. Flowers bloomed on either side of the deck, spilling bright petals around them like a private luau. Gabe had been remodeling the property for years, recently hiring a landscaper to redesign the gardens.

"Don't try to tell me there's no drinking on duty," Gabe warned him, popping the caps off with a bottle opener. "I know you're committed to being a good dad, but one beer is allowed during naptime."

"Is that right?" Damon dropped into a lounger, his eyes already moving to the beach beyond to see where Caroline and her siblings had gone.

"They're right there, Mr. Overprotective." Gabe pointed down the beach to where the four of them were dragging paddleboards onto the shore.

The two boys were having squirt gun wars at the same time, shooting each other while running for cover in the bushes that spilled onto the beach.

"I'm still getting used to life without bodyguards." Damon had let the security detail go once he knew Stephan would be in prison for good.

Or at least until his sons were over eighteen.

But after having Caroline disappear on him once, it wasn't easy relaxing his instincts.

"I know, bro." Gabe clapped him on the shoulder and then tipped his bottle to Damon's. "And you're dealing with everything like a champ."

"I don't want to be so protective I drive Caroline away." He had spent every second with her since the day she'd regained her memory, hardly daring to believe that she was back. Whole.

His.

Getting to know her all over again made every day happier than the one that came before. And seeing her as a mother made him so damn proud he thought he'd burst with it.

Gabe laughed. "Yeah. I don't think that's happening. That woman loves you something fierce."

Lifting the beer to his lips, Damon relaxed into his seat, inhaling the sea air. "I'll drink to that."

"You're a lucky man." Gabe's words were wistful, hinting at a wealth of mixed emotions beneath the surface.

Gabe's ex-wife had been pregnant when she decided she didn't want to be a mother. Soon after she gave birth, she'd walked away from the baby and left the marriage. Now, Gabe's ten-month-old son, Jason, was well-loved but motherless. Damon knew it broke his brother's heart. The boy was currently napping back at Gabe's place tended to by a nanny.

"I am, at that. Thank you for letting us crash here for a few weeks." Damon straightened in his seat, seeing Caroline head their way while Victoria retrieved a huge plastic water gun to chase her brothers. "I hope it's not…awkward."

"More than anything, I want Jason to experience having a family." Gabe picked at the beer label with his thumbnail. "You're giving him that and I'm glad about it." He peered up, seeing Caroline wrapping a towel around herself as she walked closer. "In fact, I'm so grateful, I'm going to do you a favor and keep watch on your nursery monitor if you want to take some down-time with the missus."

Damon grinned. "I've got a better idea." Getting to his feet, he held out his arms to his beautiful wife, hauling her close to kiss her cheek. "I'll keep the nursery monitor while you go show the Degraff crew how to win a squirt gun war."

Gabe raised an eyebrow. "I do have the mother of all water guns in the shed."

"I seem to remember you trying to blast me with it on my last visit."

Setting aside his empty bottle, Gabe shot to his feet. "You're on."

Caroline called after him. "Victoria is craftier than she looks."

Gabe was already out of sight when he shouted back, "I love a worthy opponent."

Damon turned his attention to the woman in his arms, still damp from her paddleboard adventure. She smelled like coconut sunscreen and sunshine; her lips were salty when he kissed her.

"Not as much as I love you," he told her. "I hope you're not getting tired of hearing that."

"I can't hear it enough." She trailed a touch along his cheek, cooling his hot skin with her fingers. "And I want to make love to you and hear you say it again and again." She kissed the words into his skin as her lips traced a path along his jaw. "But first, I want to stare into our son's crib together and marvel at what a miracle he is."

Damon's throat closed with emotion. He was a lucky man to have the love of this strong, incredible woman who'd been through so much. Who'd fought so hard to reunite their family and have a future together.

"Sounds like another perfect day."

"Another happy day," she corrected him softly. "That's all I want."

"One lifetime of happy days, coming up." Damon would move mountains to give them to her. Picking up the baby monitor, he walked with her into the bungalow to retreat from the sun. To have her all to himself for a little while. "I promise."

\* \* \* \* \*

*If you liked this story of the McNeill family,*
*pick up these other*
MCNEILL MAGNATES *books from*
*Joanne Rock!*

*THE MAGNATE'S MAIL-ORDER BRIDE*
*THE MAGNATE'S MARRIAGE MERGER*
*HIS ACCIDENTAL HEIR*
*LITTLE SECRETS: HIS PREGNANT SECRETARY*

*as well as reader favorite*
*SECRET BABY SCANDAL*
*Available now from Harlequin Desire!*

*If you're on Twitter, tell us what you think of*
*Harlequin Desire! #harlequindesire.*

# Get 2 Free Books,
## Plus 2 Free Gifts—
### just for trying the Reader Service!

HARLEQUIN *Desire*

Being so close to this man had never been a wise idea.

The sensual draw was too strong for any woman to resist for
long and stay sane. Broderick's long wool duster over his suit was
pure Hugo Boss. But the cowboy hat and leather boots had a hint of
wear that only increased his appeal. His dark hair, which attested to
his quarter-Inuit heritage, showed the first signs of premature gray.
His charisma and strength were as vast as the Alaskan tundra they
both called home.

In a state this large, there should have been enough space for
both of them. Theoretically, they should never have to cross paths.
But their feuding families' constant battle over dominance of the
oil industry kept Glenna Mikkelson-Powers and Broderick Steele
in each other's social circles.

Too often for her peace of mind.

Even so, he'd never shown up at her office before.

Light caught the mischief in his eyes, bringing out whiskey
tones in the dark depths. His full lips pulled upward in a haughty
smile.

"You're being highly unprofessional." She narrowed her own
eyes, angry at her reaction to him as she drank in his familiar
arrogance.

Their gazes held and the air crackled. She remembered the feeling all too well from their *Romeo and Juliet* fling in college.

Doomed from the start.

He was her rival. His mesmerizing eyes and broody disposition would not distract her.

She jabbed a manicured finger in his direction. "Your father is up to something."

She scooped up a brass paperweight in the shape of a bear that had belonged to her father. Shifting it from hand to hand was an oddly comforting ritual. Or perhaps not so odd. When she was a small girl, her father had told her the statue gave people power, attributing his success to the brass bear. After the last year of loss, Glenna needed every ounce of luck and power she could get.

"There's no need to threaten me with your version of brass knuckles." Humor left his face and his expression became all business. "But since you're as bemused by what's happening as I am, come with me to speak to your mother."

"Of course. Let's do that. We'll have this sorted out in no time."

The sooner the better.

She wanted Broderick Steele out of her office and not a simple touch away.

*Don't miss*
*THE BABY CLAIM*
*by* USA TODAY *bestselling author Catherine Mann,*
*the first book in the* **ALASKAN OIL BARONS** *saga!*
*Available February 2018*
*wherever Harlequin® Desire books and ebooks are sold.*

*And then follow the continuing story of two merging oil families*
*competing to win in business...and in love—*

*THE DOUBLE DEAL*
*Available March 2018*

*THE LOVE CHILD*
*Available April 2018*

*THE TWIN BIRTHRIGHT*
*Available May 2018*

www.Harlequin.com

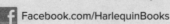